ADVENTURES OF A YOUNG MAN

BY JOHN REED

JOHN REED
Adventures
OF A YOUNG
MAN

short stories

from life

CITY LIGHTS

© 1975 by City Lights Books

Published as a Seven Seas Book 1963, 1966
Copyright Seven Seas Books

Library of Congress Cataloging in Publication Data:

Reed, John, 1887-1920
    Adventures of a young man.

    Reprint of the 1966 ed. published by Seven Seas
Publishers, Berlin, in series: Seven seas books.

    I. Title.   II. Series: Seven seas books.

PZ3.R2525Ad8   (PS3535.E2786) 813'.5'2   75-14275
ISBN 0-87286-083-3

CITY LIGHTS BOOKS are published at the City Lights
Bookstore. Editorial and publishing offices: 1562 Grant
Avenue, San Francisco, California 94133

CONTENTS

Introduction   9

AMERICANS AT HOME AND ABROAD

The Capitalist   15
Where the Heart Is   23
A Taste of Justice   30
Seeing Is Believing   34
Another Case of Ingratitude   47
Mac — American   51
The Rights of Small Nations   57
Broadway Night   62
Endymion: or On the Border   71

JOHN BULL IN AMERICA

The Thing to Do   83
The Head of the Family   89

EN ROUTE

Mexican Pictures   101
    I. Soldiers of Fortune
    II. Peons
The World Well Lost   107

REVOLUTIONARY VIGNETTES

I. On the Eve   115
II. The I.W.W. Trial at Chicago   122

■

Almost Thirty   125

PREFACE TO CITY LIGHTS EDITION 1975

The time has come around again for John Reed. We see him now through the telescope of time, one of those figures still somehow larger than life, an archetype of the American writer or radical who "went all the way" with the Bolshevik experiment of 1917 — and ended up in a grave of revolutionaries under the Kremlin Wall.

There were painted tin flowers on John Reed's grave. They have not faded, though they may have been carted in and out a few times. In February 1967 I saw a brilliant new dramatization of his *Ten Days That Shook The World* at the Drama Theatre in Moscow. Yet in the USA, in his own country he has not been such a hero much of the time since his death. Here he has often been attacked and put down for being a "playboy of the social revolution" (Upton Sinclair), for being a naive dilettante or a "sentimental imitation of Jack London" (Kenneth Rexroth).

There is indeed, in some of his descriptions of the "poor and downtrodden," a sense of the upperclass adventurer doing a little slumming. One can almost see the five-pound wingtip shoes and the Ivy League suit, one of the world's most boring costumes. And Reed did have a fatal innocence about him, a political naiveté which led directly to his death in Moscow. "On earth they were building a kingdom," he wrote from there in 1917, "more bright than any heaven had to offer, and for which it was a glory to die." He did. But when he did, he muttered over and over, "Caught in a trap, caught in a trap." He had painted himself into that corner which a whole generation of American radicals was to paint itself into — that of the totalitarian State which refused to "wither away" as it was supposed to.

Yet Reed's time has come again because his writing

7

also embodies that still insurgent spirit in American life which is much closer to Whitman than to Lenin. (Reed in fact knew Whitman's writing better.) This insurgent spirit is more anarchist and libertarian than authoritarian. It is the spirit of his fiction, not his political reportage, and yet this fiction has generally been considered beneath notice, and no American publisher saw fit to print these stories in the decade since they were published abroad. What also comes through to us in them is a gusto and a love-of-life, an acute and often euphoric observation of the world, coupled with the defiance of youth. And we can use this kind of native solar energy today, in this too-cool post-SLA "time of the ostrich."

To these stories (originally gathered together by Seven Seas Publishers in Berlin and published with a party-line Introduction) we have added "Almost Thirty," Reed's assessment of himself looking back over the years in which most of these stories were written. It evidently wasn't published until the *New Republic* picked it up in 1936, nineteen years later, and it has never appeared in book form.

—Lawrence Ferlinghetti

INTRODUCTION

These stories by the youthful John Reed evoke a pang of sorrow that he died in the early flower of his many-sided brilliance. He was not yet thirty-three years old, this American whose body lay in state in Moscow in the winter of 1920 guarded by soldiers of the young Red Army. He was best known then, as today, for his classic eye-witness history of the Soviet Revolution, *Ten Days That Shook the World*. What more he might have given the world will never be known.

How John Reed developed from the "universally acclaimed wonder-boy" who came out of Harvard in 1910, into the man who wrote that masterpiece of literary reportage, has been kept successfully hidden by the American Establishment. How successfully can be judged to some extent by the fact that most people know him only as the author of *Ten Days*, and not as one of the world's great short-story writers.

Such stories as appear in this volume have been quietly and effectively suppressed. It is not surprising. Reed lived in turbulent times and he rode the waves with zest and emotion. He had the drive to discover and the sharp eye of a poet to observe. More, he had the integrity and human compassion to face the deep meaning of what he saw so clearly.

His character showed early — even before he himself was aware of it. One of his Harvard classmates, later a Wall Street lawyer, wrote that Reed did not "know the difference between cricket and not-cricket." It was not true. He sensed the difference well enough but at that time he did not know that there were two teams with different rules. He only saw — with the poet's eye, with lack of fear and with integrity. And though he was brilliant, though he led in every sphere from water polo to drama, the Harvard machine made sure that he never entered its select circles.

He shot into journalism like a star as soon as he left Harvard. His name was a byword. Newspapers and magazines competed for the flood of stories, reports and articles that gushed from his fertile brain. But the earliest of the stories in this selection – written in 1912 and ironically titled *The Capitalist* – shows why it was no accident that he forsook easy money to join the group of rebellious writers and artists who were then launching *The Masses*.

In 1913 came the great strike of textile workers in Paterson, New Jersey. This was the second phase of his education.

He met the strikers – dour and resolute and yet full of spirit like himself – worked with the organizer of the "Wobblies," the Industrial Workers of the World, was arrested and returned to New York where he produced the hot-blooded Paterson strike pageant in Madison Square Garden.

To his Harvard classmates this was betrayal. To the strikers who battled for a wage it was truth. It was at once cricket and not-cricket.

Late in 1913 he went to Mexico where he took sides with Villa, lived with his soldiers and accompanied them into battle. From these reports and from his book *Insurgent Mexico* he won more fame – a fame that ensured his being sent to Europe at the outbreak of the First World War.

For so far, not all of the cricketers had discovered that he was a cuckoo in the nest. Nor perhaps had John Reed himself. In Europe during the early war years he was still the journalist for whom the cash-on-the-nail press clamored, a star, accepted as the greatest American war correspondent. But it is enough to read *Mac – American, The Rights of Small Nations, The Thing to Do* and *The Head of the Family* in this collection to see why his writings steadily lost their glamour for a pro-war press.

He was still writing for the *Metropolitan Magazine* for his wages and for *The Masses* in order to write as he felt, but it was a feat he could not long continue. By 1916, he was taking an ever more active part against "this traders' war" in his poetry, articles, stories and plays. He had become a definite non-cricketer and the popular press which had competed for his work dropped him completely. Harvard men cut him on the street.

It seems quite natural that his fine, sensitive nose for life should have led him to be on the spot in 1917 when the Soviet Revolution took place. Again, history had curiously conspired to have the right man at the right place at the right time. All that he had ever done came to his aid in that masterpiece of objective analysis. *Ten Days* has stood since that time as the outstanding account of the October Revolution.

John Reed returned to the United States quite changed by that experience. Events had convinced him that the only path for human advance was from capitalism to socialism and that this required the existence of a party able to lead the workers and to organize resistance to armed reaction.

He underscored the lessons of *Ten Days* in meetings all over the United States and was arrested half a dozen times. By now the boycott by the popular press was absolute and he poured out articles for the left press. The reckless youth who had left Harvard became a patient, meticulous organizer and one of the leaders of the Communist Labor Party when it was founded in 1919. Back in the Soviet Union in 1920, he was welcomed as a man who had fought to establish the truth about this crossroads of history and as a member of the executive committee of the Communist International. He died there of typhus on October 17, 1920, and was buried near the Kremlin Wall.

As to what kind of man John Reed was — this far from

quiet American — these stories help us to know. Whatever else he may hide, no writer can hide himself from a penetrating reader. In this collection one sees the young John Reed, still raffish and immature but moved by those qualities which in the end could only take him along the road he took, the man so early recognized by the budding lawyer as a non-cricketer in the Wall Street team.

Here is his descriptive ability, the compact, tight, poetic use of words; the gaiety and adventure, always with an eye razor-sharp for human relations; tenderness without saccharine; compassion without false pity and above all the love of life and people.

To these short stories have been added *The World Well Lost, Mexican Pictures*, taken from press accounts of his Mexican adventures, *Revolutionary Vignettes*, snatches of description of a visit to the Riga front shortly before the October Revolution and an extract from a report of the I.W.W. trial in 1918. They were published in 1927 by the Vanguard Press, Inc., with the permission of Louise Bryant, John Reed's wife.

It has been said often that there is no better way to a first understanding of the Soviet Revolution than through John Reed's magnificent report — throbbing with accurately observed detail which brings to life the time, the events and their significance. Perhaps it is also true that there is no better way to understanding how he became what he was than by reading these stories, written in those youthful, formative years when life is an adventure.

SEVEN SEAS PUBLISHERS

Berlin, 1966

AMERICANS
AT HOME
AND ABROAD

THE CAPITALIST

You know how Washington Square looks in a wet mist on November nights; that gray, luminous pastel atmosphere, softening incredibly the hard outlines of bare trees and iron railings, obliterating the sharp edges of shadows, and casting a silver halo about each high electric globe. All the straight concrete walks are black onyx, jeweled in every little unevenness with pools of steely rain-water. An imperceptible rain fills the air; your cheeks and the backs of your hands are damp and cool. And yet you can walk three times around the Square with your raincoat open, and not get wet at all.

It was on such a night that William Booth Wrenn, strolling from somewhere to nowhere in particular, stopped under the two arc-lights near Washington Arch to count his wealth. It was almost midnight. William Booth Wrenn had just received his compensation for doing – no matter what. It amounted to sixty-five cents in all. This was the third time he had counted it.

A hasty glance at Mr. Wrenn, if you are not particularly observant, would have convinced you that he was an ordinary young man in ordinary circumstances, perhaps a clerk in some flourishing haberdashery shop. His tan shoes showed traces of a recent shine, his hat was of a formless English cloth, and his raincoat was the right length. There was an air about him as of a young man who knew how to wear his clothes. The indulgent mist aided this impression. One must appear so if one is hunting a job in New York. But if you had looked closer, you might have noticed that his high collar was frayed and smudgy-looking; if you could have peered beneath his coat, you would have seen that the collar was attached to a mere sleeveless rag that was no shirt at all; if you could have examined the soles of his shoes, you would have discovered two gaping holes there, a pair of drenched socks coming through. How were you to know that the raincoat was "slightly damaged by fire" within? Or that the English hat was fast ungluing in the wet?

After reckoning up his resources, William flipped a coin in the air. It came heads; he took the right-hand path across the Square, jingling the coins in his pocket.

Between two arc-lights on that path there is a dreary stretch of hard wooden benches. In the dim light, he made out two persons occupying opposite sides of the walk. One was a sodden bundle of a drunkard, uncomfortably draped across the iron arm rests which the city rivets there to prevent tired, homeless people from sleeping. His bloated face was turned blindly skyward, and he snored raspingly. Tiny drops of water thickly encrusted him, twinkling as his chest rose and fell. The other occupant was an old woman. A strong odor of whiskey emanated from her. A green cheesecloth scarf, glistening with dew, transversed her scant gray hair, and was knotted under her chin. She sang:

Oh, I know my love (hic) by his way o' walkin' (hic),
I (hic) know my love by his way o' (hic) talkin',
And I know my (hic) love by his coat o' blu-u-u-e,
And if my love left me (hic) –

At that, she seemed to hear the jingling of William's coins, and suddenly broke off, saying:

"C'mere!"

William stopped, turned, lifted his hat with a courtly gesture.

"I beg your pardon, madam!"

"C'mere! I said."

He sat beside her on the bench and peered curiously into her face. It was extraordinarily lined and drawn, withered like the faces of very old scrubwomen that one sometimes sees after hours in office buildings; the lower lip trembled senilely. She turned a pair of glazed, faded eyes upon him.

"Gawd damn your soul!" said she. "Ain't (hic) ain't you got better manners 'n to jingle yer money at that fellow an' me?"

William smiled.

"But, my good woman – " he began in his best manner.

"Good woman (hic) be cursed to you!" said the old lady. "I know ye – you rich fellers. I bet ye never worked one minute for yer money – yer father left it to ye – now didn't he? I thought so. I know ye – " She sought the right word: "ye Capitalist!"

A pleasant glow of satisfaction pervaded William. He nodded complacently.

"How'd you guess?"

"Guess!" laughed the woman unpleasantly. "Guess! (hic). Don't ye think *I* worked in fine houses? Don't ye think *I* had rich young fellers – when I was a young gurrul? *Know* ye? Wid yer jinglin' money an' yer dainty manners! What one o' ye would take off yer hat (hic) to 'n old souse like me – if you weren't jokin'?"

"Madam, I assure you – "

"My Gawd! *Listen* to 'm! Aw, yes; many's the fine rich young lover (hic) I had when I was a young gurrul. They took off their hats *then* – "

William wondered if this hideous old ruin had ever been beautiful. It stimulated his imagination.

When I was a young (hic) gurrul –

Oh, I know my love –

"Say-y-y-y ... I was a-thinkin' when I heard that money jinglin' – Ain't it funny how ye jingle everything ye get? You do – I do – everybody does. I say, I was a-thinkin' (hic) wouldn't you like to come along with me and have some fun?" She leaned over and leered at him in awful burlesque of her youth; the smell of bad whiskey fouled his nostrils. "C'mon! Give you a goo – (hic) good time, dear. Wan' go somewhere have some fun?"

"No, thank you. Not tonight," answered William gently.

"Sure," sneered the old lady. "*I* know ye, ye Cap'tal'sts! Give us work w'en we don't want it. But ye won't give 's work w'en we (hic) want it. Take yer hand out o' yer pocket! *I* won't take yer dirty charity.... Had enough charity. I *work* fer what I get. See? (hic) No decent woman'd take yer charity.... C'mon, give ye a good – "

"Why are you sitting out here? You'll catch cold – "

"Why you – Wot t'ell do ye think I'm sittin' out here for? I just can't stay 'n my boodwar these here fine summer evenin's! If I got paid fer wot I done, think I'd be sittin' out here? Jesus!" she blazed out at him furiously. "You b'long to the City?"

William shook his head. He drew from his pocket a cheap cigarette box, and opened it. There were two cigarettes.

"Do you mind if I smoke?" he asked politely. The old lady stared at him.

"Do I mind if you smoke! What t'ell d'you want, young feller? Why d'ye ask me w'ether you c'n smoke? W'at business is it o' mine w'ether you – Sure, I'll take one – " He struck a match.

"Yer a Cap'tal'st," she went on, the cigarette trem-

bling in her lips. "Ye wouḷdn't be so p'lite to *me* if you
didn't want sumpin'.... *I* know ye.... You don' b'long
to the City. If you did, you'd be gettin' paid. I don't get
paid an' I (hic) belong t' the City.... Look at this here."
She fumbled in the bosom of her dress, and produced a
card. Stooping as to catch the rays of the arc-light, he read:

*Pass Mrs. Sara Trimball for one month from date to
Randall's Island. To visit daughter.*

"That's me," said Mrs. Trimball, with a kind of alco-
holic pride. "I work up t' Ran'all's Island – sort of git-
along-there-do-this-do-that fer the nurses 'n' doctors (hic).
We get paid today. I come all the way down to the City
Hall. Get there at fi' minutes past three, 'n I don't get
m' money! Y'un'erstand? Don't get *any* money till next
Friday (hic). Ain't that hell? The nurses an' doctors they
get *their* money up t' five 'clock.... W'y can't I get my
money? *They* know I ain't got no place t' sleep.... W'y?
So I say (hic) 'aw-right,' an' go sleep in park. Jus' b'fore
you come, a big cop says, 'git out o' here!' City won't pay
me w'at I work fer.... I go sleep in City Park.... City
cop comes an' drives me 'way.... Where'll I go? Go t'
the devil! Ain't that a round o' pleasure (hic)?"

"You have a daughter there?"

"Sure I got a daughter.... Sixteen years old. Here's
'nother funny thing (hic). If I didn't work up there, I c'd
keep 'er there fer nawthin'. But I work up there, an' it
costs me two dollars a week to keep her there."

"Why do you work up there?" William protested
loftily. "That's criminal extravagance for a poor person
like you – "

"Hear 'm talk, the dirty loafer – !" she responded with
heat. "Don't ye think I wan' to *see* 'er sometimes? O
Gawd, what *do* I do 't fer? She ought to be out on the
streets, earnin' enough to take care o' me in my old age."

"Of course she ought. It's ridiculous – "

"*I* don' know w'y I keep her shut away like that. . . . There ain't (hic) any sense to it. Will ye tell me w'y I don' want my kid to be like me? *I* always had a good time – *I* always lived happy. . . . W'y don't we want our kids to be like us? She ought to be out workin' fer me – but I go on keepin' her there, so she won't be like me. . . . W'at difference does it make (hic)? W'en I'm gone she'll have to, anyhow. . . ." Mrs. Trimball began to cough, slightly at first and then more violently, until her whole body was wrenched. The mist came steadily down. William felt the subtle chill of it stealing through his body. The sleeper across the way suddenly swallowed a prodigious snore, sneezed, and slowly sat up.

"Why can't ye let a guy sleep?" he mumbled. "All that dam' coughin' –"

"O Gawd!" said Mrs. Trimball weakly, the paroxysm past. "I wish I had a drink."

"How much does a room cost?" asked William.

"A quarter. You wan' a room? I know a good place right down Fourth Street. . . . Naw, w'at you givin' us? *You* don' want no room. . . ."

"No, but *you* do. Wait a minute please! I'm not going to offer you charity." He held out a quarter. "You can borrow it from me. I'd do the same with you, you know – and you can pay me back when you get paid." He dropped it into her shaking hand. She clutched at it and missed. The coin clinked upon the pavement and rolled. Quick as light a long, ragged arm shot out from the opposite bench, and the sleeper was reeling away down the path with his precious find.

Mrs. Trimball half rose from her seat. "You drunken bum!" she screamed shrilly. "Come back with that, you dirty thief – !"

"Never mind," said William, his arm on hers. "There's plenty more at home like that. Here's another." This time she clutched it.

"I'm thankin' you very much," said Mrs. Trimball with dignity. "Between friends borrowin's all right (hic). I'll ask ye to give me your name an' address, and I'll return it to you." She fumbled in her bag and produced a much-bitten pencil and a letter. "Perhaps you might be able to put another dime on that, so's I can get a drop to warm me stomach."

William hesitated only for an instant. "Certainly," he agreed. Then he set his wits to work, conjuring up all his remembrances of the Society Page in the Sunday papers. He wrote upon the letter:

Courcey de Peyster Stuyvesant
Hotel Plaza

"Didn't I tell ye?" cried the old lady as he orated this. "I know ye (hic). *I'll* have no truck wid ye! You gettin' yer money from yer pa, and me workin' on me knees seven days out o' the week. Ain't that a hell of a name to have wished on ye? Are ye ashamed to walk a few steps with an ol' souse like me, Mr. Cursey Dee Pyster Stuyvesant?"

"Not at all. A pleasure, I assure you." William rose stiffly to his feet and took the old lady's arm. He shivered. It seemed as if standing up exposed to the chill other parts of his body that had been fairly warm while he remained seated.

"Look at us!" remarked Mrs. Trimball. "Here we all elect a President of the United States . . . the very feller that promises to make everything all right (hic). I say, here we elect a President, an' all we get is – Police. . . ."

William bluffed magnificently. "But, my dear lady, we *must* safeguard Society. . . ."

Mrs. Trimball turned at her door. "You're a good young feller for a Cap'tal'st. You got the stuff in you. All you want is a little hard work. . . ."

"If you working people weren't so extravagant, you'd save enough to make you comfortable in your old age. . . ."

21

William Booth Wrenn walked back into the Square. His feet were without feeling, but the dampness had worked through his thin clothing and all his body was damp and chilled. He sought the bench he had just quitted, fingering the nickel in his pocket. In a dry corner underneath the seat, between the iron and the wood, he found the stump of his cigarette. After four trials, a damp match was induced to splutter into blue flame. He lighted the tobacco, drawing a long breath of it into his lungs, and warmed his hands over the match.

Just then a well-nourished, cape-muffled policeman appeared, motioning with his club.

"Move on," he said briefly. "You can't sit here."

William took another puff at his snipe, and, without moving, drawled insolently, "My man, do you know who I am?"

The policeman took in the dirty collar, the cheap hat, the wet shoes. Policemen's eyes are sharper than old ladies'. Then he leaned forward and peered into William's face.

"Yes," he said, "I know who you are. You're the guy that I chased out of here twice already last night. Now git, or I'll fan you!"

1912

WHERE THE HEART IS

Two!" barks the giant in the aged dinner-coat, over your shoulders to the ticket window. He is grizzled and massive, with a face like a Roman senator; his hand closes belligerently over your tickets as he surveys you keenly to see if you're drunk. Then you push open the always-swinging, colored-glass doors, and the lights and movement, the blatant dance-rhythm of the Haymarket hits you like a physical blow.

Bill the Bouncer, also informally dressed, leans against the brass rail which fences you off from the main floor, and grins at you like a prize fighter, if you know him; otherwise he takes your measure with a surly nod. Bill stands for the proprieties. Woe to the youthful collegian who bursts into song. Woe to the elderly rake whose manners are anything but conventional. Woe also to the dancer who frolics, or the girl who dares to outrage decency by smoking cigarettes in public.* The Haymarket is the most respectable place in town.

It is all too brightly lighted, reflected from mirrors along the wall; there is utterly unlimited crash from the

* 1912

23

brazen orchestra, metallic tones of conversations curiously off-key from the ordinary human voice, female figures in impossible caricatures of the extreme mode, men and women waltzing slowly on the crowded floor in every unnatural posture ... round wooden tables everywhere, and the continuous stream of derby hats moving in and out of the place. As you stop and try to reduce these varied impressions to some sort of order, you will suddenly feel Eyes upon you; all over the hall, from tables right near the rail, from seats in the gallery, girls.are watching steadily each new arrival; girls pretty, hideous, badly dressed, gorgeously dressed, but never poorly dressed. They do not invite, those eyes, nor challenge, nor say evil things. They simply watch you steadily, hungrily, as a cat watches a mouse.

So I came into the Haymarket after many months. It was the same that it always had been. "Bill," I said, "it's good to see you." And it was. "Is Martha here?"

Bill nodded – he is a man of few words – and jerked a thumb toward the rear room. But even there – a place of yellow play-bills and photographs of dead-and-gone burlesques, and the inevitable tables, each with its girl – I failed to find her. Of course she might have changed. . . . I didn't go upstairs to the balcony, however, but went through one of the doors that give.onto the dancing-floor, and sat at a table. A waiter came, and I whispered to him. And a few moments later I saw a woman rise and move across the hall toward me. It was Martha, slender, dressed in a dark blue suit, with a dull yellow plume on her hat.

"Hello dear," she said. That's the manner of greeting in the Haymarket. Then she gave me a small hand, smiled decorously, and sat down. I noticed that her hair was still soft and dark, her face oval and delicately colored, her eyes honest and unclouded.

We ordered beer.

"Why," she said suddenly, "I've seen you before."

"Not for four years," I told her. "I knew you."

"Oh, yes," her eyes lit up like an old friend's. "In the old days. May Munro was here then, and Laura Chevalier and Babe Taylor. All the old crowd. I guess I'm the only one left of the bunch."

"Tell me what you've been doing with yourself all this time."

She shrugged her shoulders. "Nothing much. Same. . . . O, now you wait! I guess I've been to Europe since I saw you last."

"Europe!" I said, wondering. She nodded, smiling. The dancing had ended for the moment, and on the tawdry stage two men and a woman sang a song about the "Turkey Trot," yelling at the top of their voices and beating a drum and cymbals. The obvious, sordid chords of the music jarred fearfully with the mangled voices. The noise was deafening. The singers' bodies moved from the hips in nervous, grotesque rhythm. There was something brutally abandoned and not unpleasant about it – something that chimed in with hard-eyed, artificial women and mirrors. They sang "It's a bear! It's a bear! It's a bear!"

"That certainly is a good song," murmured Martha, dreamy-eyed. "Well, about Europe – D'y'ever go there?"

"Yes." I smiled. "I suppose you saw the Moulin Rouge and the Abbaye, and the Globe in London?"

"No, I didn't go around to many of the sporting places. Seen enough of that."

"Martha," I said, curious, "what did you go abroad for?"

She frowned. "Well, I wanted to learn something. You know how you've got a lot of things in your head that you got out of school books when you was a kid; like the Tower of London, and Shakespeare's house at Stratford. Well, you believe they're *there* all right, but you have to *see* 'em to know for sure."

It was something of a shock. But, after all, why shouldn't

a Haymarket girl want to see Shakespeare's house like other people? ...

She went on: "I always saved my money. Don't know why, unless it was to buy a little cottage out in the country some day, and keep chickens. I'm going to do that when I get all in. Last spring I got to thinking. An' so one day I drew my money out of the bank an' bought a new suit an' took the *Lusitania* – first cabin. No, you can bet I'm no cheap skate."

"But did you have enough money – ?"

Martha laughed. "Only enough to get to London and stay there like a real tourist for a week. No, of course I didn't know what would happen to me after that. Just trusted to Gawd. On the boat I met a nice couple of old boneheads – preacher and his wife, I guess – and went down to London with 'em. Say, they were certainly good people – thought I was a college girl. I always dress quiet, you know. I like it. A girl who dresses loud is in bad from the start. We put up at the Waldorf in London – quiet an' respectable as hell – an' the three of us certainly did that town. London Bridge, Westminster, Crystal Palace; we laid out the burg in sections. Some tourists, believe me! O, sure I went to the Alhambra and the Globe, when the chaperonies were pounding their ear. But the English girls are awful snobs."

She mused reminiscently. "I'll never forget that week. Good time? Say, I acted like a kid about two years old. Seein' all the things you'd heard about."

Beyond us the band crashed into the braying "Gaby Glide." Bill the Bouncer leaned threateningly on the rail. I had once seen him drag a girl, who had stabbed a waiter with her hatpin, across the floor, and throw her bodily through the outer door. Right near us was a table at which sat a young, fresh girl timidly talking to a derby hat – flushing and paling. A new one. . . . But I was intent upon Martha's adventure. Alone in London – *learning*.

"But what did you do for money?" I asked realistically.

"I'm coming to that. One morning I woke up with seven shillings. An' that day a young American spoke to me when I was killing time in Hyde Park. I was getting sort of doped with London, anyway. So that night I kissed the old lady good night, went up to my room an' packed. We lit out at two in the morning. I've often wondered what she thought next day. So that's how I went to Paris. We certainly lived like two kings in the Grand Hotel. Say, did you ever sit on the sidewalk in front of one of those cafés about five o'clock, an' see the birds parade up and down? That for mine. You feel kind o' lazy. I bet I wore out three pair of shoes tramping through the Loover, with a catalogue in my mitt. The fellow? O, he was all right. Bought me nifty dresses – you should've seen the black silk. Nothing flashy, though. Lots of American girls in Paris have to live. I was in Paris two weeks, an' one day my friend beat it. I would 'a' been on the street in another day if I hadn't run into the Englishman. . . .

"He was about sixty years old an' had a stomach – but he certainly treated me white. We traveled up through Belgium and Holland; Brussels, The Hague, Ostend, then took a trip through Germany. I never missed a trick. Up at Waterloo I spent a whole day reading a history book. It seemed to me as if I was itching until I'd seen everything in the Baydicker. But after a while, when we got around to Strassburg, he began to get sore. 'Look here,' he says to me, 'chop the Cook Tourist stuff, can't you?' So I simply cleared out one night and left him. I wasn't going to be anybody's dog, you bet! Just had money enough to get to Paris. . . . But I knew nothing could happen to me with *my* luck. The very first night I went up on Monmarter an' ran into an American girl who let me sleep in her bed. All us American girls stick by each other, you know. Sure, I went to all the joints. Monmarter is just like New York,

27

except it isn't so *honest,* if you know what I mean. Well, say, of all the luck! The very next night in Pigalle's I danced with a man that looked like a half-coon, only he wasn't. Nobody is, over there. An' he gave me his card an' asked me to go to Brazil with him. The card had a little crown on it, an' *Count Manuel da Portales.*

"I'd heard a lot about bogus counts, and so forth, putting one over on poor girls; so when I saw Mabel I showed her the card, and asked her if he was a fake. 'Go to it,' she says. 'Take a chance!' But even then I wasn't satisfied. I didn't get any sleep that night, you can believe *me.* Suppose he'd take me somewhere where I didn't know the language and nobody talked American, and leave me? But I trusted to Gawd and went. It took us two weeks on the boat – then Rio. I guess Rio's the most beautiful place in the world. I had a great time there. Every Friday night we'd go to the High-Life Club for dinner, an' Saturday after supper the whole town would put on costumes – fancy dress, you know – and ride up an' down in hacks. I stayed there four months. . . .

"No, I wasn't very happy. You see, you get tired of wondering at things. Everything in foreign countries is so much finer than you ever thought it would be. Then you get excited when you see something you've always heard about. It kind of gets on your nerves, and takes it out of you. I was going to stick around Rio for a year. But I didn't. . . .

"I can remember just as plain. One night we came in rather tight after a big party at the club. Manuel dropped off to sleep, but I couldn't seem to close my eyes. It was in April, and the window was open, an' I could see straight up about a million miles in the sky. The stars are bear-cats down there. I don't know what got me to thinking about Broadway, but right off the bat I seemed to see it, wrigglin' and squirmin' with electric signs; with all the low-brows coming out of the moving-picture shows, an' the shirt fronts comin' out of the Theayter – the hurdy-gurdies playing that 'Irish Rag' at that moment. I was as sick as a hound for old, honest, low-brow New York! You see, in foreign countries everybody is a high-brow. Then I saw the old Market, with all the girls sitting around, an' the beer-stains on the table, an' the Sweet Cap cigarette smoke. About then all the college boys would be down for their vacation, an' of course come roaming into the Market. I began to feel real tender about Big Bill there. So I gave Manuel a poke. 'What's a matter?' says he. 'I've got a cablegram from New York,' says I. 'It's very important. Coney Island will open on the first. When's the next boat?' I says. 'I'm going to breeze.'

"I will say the Count was O. K. He bought me a first. That trip up the coast was the best time I ever had in my life. I lived strictly alone; didn't allow a man on board to get fresh. Just read books; didn't talk to any one. . . .

"Well, from the first minute I began to see the old town loom up the bay, I was so excited I couldn't talk. It hurt. I didn't wait for anything. When we landed I checked my stuff in the Erie station and took a ferry. Then I took the L to Twenty-eighth Street and blew in here. The old gink outside says, 'Here, you can't walk in here without a ticket' – an' then he looked closer. 'Well, what the . . . Say, where have you been?' I couldn't answer him. I stood there like a deaf and dumb and blind bonehead – I was so absolutely off my nut. An' he held the door open an' I sort of *fell* inside. There was Bill, and behind him all the crowd was dancing, and the little tables. Home! That's what it was! Home!

"I heard the Big Fellow rumbling 'Martha! By God! The Female White Hope has come back!'

"O Gawd! You couldn't understand. I just fell on a table and bawled. . . . Come on, let's dance."

1913

29

A TASTE OF JUSTICE

As soon as the dark sets in, young girls begin to pass that Corner – squat-figured, hard-faced, "cheap" girls, like dusty little birds wrapped too tightly in their feathers. They come up Irving Place from Fourteenth Street, turn back toward Union Square on Sixteenth, stroll down Fifteenth (passing the Corner again) to Third Avenue, and so around – always drawn back to the Corner. By some mysterious magnetism, the Corner of Fifteenth Street and Irving Place fascinates them. Perhaps that particular spot means Adventure, or Fortune, or even Love. How did it come to have such significance? The men know that this is so; at night each shadow in the vicinity contains its derby hat, and a few bold spirits even stand in the full glare of the arc-light. Brushing against them, luring with their swaying hips, whispering from immovable lips the shocking intimacies that Business has borrowed from Love, the girls pass.

The place has its inevitable Cop. He follows the same general beat as the girls do, but at a slower, more majestic pace. This he does by keeping the girls perpetually walking – to create the illusion that they're going somewhere. Society allows vice no rest. If women stood still, what would become of us all? When the Cop appears on the Corner, the women who are lingering there scatter like a shoal of fish; and until he moves on, they wait in the dark side streets. Suppose he caught one? "The Island for hers! That's the place they cut off a girl's hair!" But the policeman is a good sport. He employs no treachery, but simply stands a moment, proudly twirling his club, and then moves down toward Fourteenth Street. It gives him an immense satisfaction to see the girls scatter.

His broad back retreats in the gloom, and the girls return – crossing and recrossing, passing and repassing with tireless feet.

Standing on that Corner, watching the little comedy, my ears were full of low whisperings, and the soft scuff of their feet. They cursed at me, or guyed me, according to whether or not they had had any dinner. And then came the Cop.

His ponderous shoulders came rolling out of the gloom of Fourteenth Street, with the satisfied arrogance of an absolute monarch. Soundlessly the girls vanished and the Corner contained but three living things; the hissing arclight, the Cop and myself.

He stood for a moment, juggling his club, and peering sullenly around. He seemed discontented about something; perhaps his conscience was troubling him. Then his eye fell on me, and he frowned.

"Move on!" he ordered, with an imperial jerk of the head.

"Why?" I asked.

"Never mind why. Because I say go. Come on now." He moved slowly in my direction.

"I'm doing nothing," said I. "I know of no law that prevents a citizen from standing on the corner, so long as he doesn't hold up traffic."

"Chop it!" rumbled the Cop, waving his club suggestively at me, "Now git along, or I'll fan ye!"

I perceived a middle-aged man hurrying along with a bundle under his arm.

"Hold on," I said; and then to the stranger, "I beg your pardon, but would you mind witnessing this business?"

"Sure," he remarked cheerfully. "What's the row?"

"I was standing inoffensively on this corner, when this officer ordered me to move on. I don't see why I should move on. He says he'll beat me with his club if I don't. Now, I want you to witness that I am making no resistance. If I've been doing anything wrong, I demand that I be arrested and taken to the Night Court." The Cop removed his helmet and scratched his head dubiously.

"That sounds reasonable." The stranger grinned. "Want my name?"

But the Cop saw the grin. "Come on then," he growled, taking me roughly by the arm. The stranger bade us good-night and departed, still grinning. The Cop and I went up Fifteenth Street, neither of us saying anything. I could see that he was troubled and considered letting me go. But he gritted his teeth and stubbornly proceeded.

We entered the dingy respectability of the Night Court, passed through a side corridor, and came to the door that gives onto the railed space where criminals stand before the Bench. The door was open, and I could see beyond the bar a thin scattering of people on the benches – sight-seers, the morbidly curious, an old Jewish woman with a brown wig, waiting, waiting, with her eyes fixed upon the door through which prisoners appear. There were the usual few lights high in the lofty ceiling, the dark, ugly paneling of imitation mahogany, that is meant to impress, and only succeeds in casting a gloom. It seems that Justice must always shun the light.

There was another prisoner before me, a slight, girlish figure that did not reach the shoulder of the policeman who held her arm. Her skirt was wrinkled and indiscriminate, and clung too closely about her hips; her shoes were cracked and too large; an enormous limp willow plume topped her off. The Judge lifted a black-robed arm – I could not hear what he said.

"Soliciting," said the hoarse voice of the policeman, "Sixth Av'nue near Twenty-third – "

"Ten days on the Island – next case."

The girl threw back her head and laughed insolently.

"You – " she shrilled, and laughed again. But the Cop thrust her violently before him, and they passed out the other door.

And I went forward with her laughter sounding in my ears.

The Judge was writing something on a piece of paper. Without looking up he snapped:

"What's the charge, officer?"

"Resisting an officer," said the Cop surlily. "I told him to move on and he says he wouldn't – "

"Hum," murmured the Judge abstractedly, still writing. "Wouldn't, eh? Well, what have you got to say for yourself?"

I did not answer.

"Won't talk, eh? Well, I guess you'll get – "

Then he looked up, nodded, and smiled.

"Hello, Reed!" he said. He venomously regarded the Cop. "Next time you pull a friend of mine – " suggestively, he left the threat unfinished. Then to me, "Want to sit up on the Bench for a while?"

1913

SEEING IS BELIEVING

Whether the girl was straight or not, George doesn't know yet. It's a thing you can usually detect in a five minutes' conversation – or anyway, George can. And this case is more important because George has rather settled ideas about that sort of thing. He is an attractive, more than usually kind-hearted fellow, who has been known to yield to our common weakness for women, and yet who has strict ideas about the position of such creatures in the social scale. I may add that he is abnormally sensitive to attempts upon his money and sympathy, and knows all the tricks.

It seems that he came out of his club on Forty-fourth Street just as a girl strolled past. She was a very small girl with fluffy hair, dressed in a cheap blue tailor suit and a round little hat with a feather sticking straight up. Now, it's usual for women to stroll down Forty-fourth Street; but it certainly isn't the appropriate promenade for small, shabby girls dressed in mail-order clothes. I wonder the police didn't stop her.

Anyway, there she was; and as George came through the swinging door, she slowed her pace very obviously and grinned at him. Now comes the most amazing part of the story: George fell into step beside her and walked along. That may not seem extraordinary to you – but then, you don't belong to a Forty-fourth street club. Why, we *never* pick up a girl in front of our club. It was the first time George had ever done it, either; and now that he looks back at it, he says that the girl must have hypnotized him from the first.

"Going anywhere in particular?" he asked, according to the formula.

She looked up at him frankly, and he noticed, all of a sudden, how extraordinarily innocent her eyes were.

"Yes," she answered, giggling a little. "I'm going with you." She caught her breath, and George wondered for the first time, if any of his friends would see him. "I've been walking most all night, except I went into the ladies' room at Macy's and slept two hours before they saw me."

"What do you want?" asked George, putting his hand in his pocket, and by this time pretty much ashamed of walking on the streets with her.

She didn't answer, and he raised his eyes to find hers filled with tears. She stopped right in the middle of the sidewalk, and turned to face him squarely, shaking her small head solemnly to and fro.

"No," she said. "No. I don't want you to pay me for letting you go. I want to talk to you."

Now, if George had been his rational self, he would have either hurled indignantly away, or taken her to one of those hotels in which the region abounds. They were within a few steps of Sixth Avenue. But some entirely new feeling made him blush (George blushing!), and instead he heard himself say: "Let's go over to the waiting-room of the Grand Central Station. We can talk there." So they faced around and walked back past the club toward Fifth Avenue. Killing, isn't it?

I can imagine them as they went along rather silently – George uncomfortable at the thought of being seen with her, and unaccountably angry with himself for being so, and perhaps wondering what kind she was; and she with chin lifted, seeming to drink in the air and the bustle around her, her gaze fixed on the tops of buildings. It had turned out one of those blue, steely days of early winter.

George kept stealing glances at her out of the corner of his eye. He was curious, and yet there were few things one could ask this girl.

"Live in New York?" he asked. It was perfectly evident that she didn't.

"W-e-ell," she hesitated. "Not just. I came here from Chillicothe, Ohio. But I like it here – awfully. The skyscrapers do tickle you so, don't they?"

"Tickle?"

"Oh, you know," she explained. "When you lean back and look up at 'em, with their high towers all gold above the highest birds, something just prickles and bubbles in you, and you laugh," and she gave a sort of ecstatic little chirp.

"I see," he murmured, more at sea than ever.

"You know, that's all I came for," she went on. "That and the millions of people."

"You mean you came to New York to see the crowds and the skyscrapers?" asked George, sarcastically. You see, George was too wise for that kind of talk.

She nodded. "It seems to me that all my life I heard nothing but New York. Every time a drummer used to come into Simond's – Simond's is where I worked, you know – or when Mr. Petty went East for the fall stock, they used to talk about the Elevated, and the Subway, and the skyscrapers, and Broadway, and – oh, they used to talk so I couldn't sleep thinking of the towers and the roaring and the lights. And so here I am – "

"But how – "

"O, I know it seems funny to you a girl like me would

have money enough to come," she said, with birdlike nods of her little head. "But you see I'm seventeen now, and I began to save when I was eleven. I saved fifty dollars."

At this moment they passed through the eastern door to the great Concourse.

George shot at her rudely: "How much have you got now?"

"Nothing," she replied; and then the marble terrace, and the gracious flight of steps, and the mighty ceiling of the starry sky, with the mystic golden procession of the Zodiac marching across it, burst upon her sight. "Oh!" she cried, and gripped the marble balustrade hard with her stubby fingers. "This is the beautifullest thing I ever saw in my life!"

"Never mind that!" George said, taking her by the arm. "You come along. I want to talk to you." She could hardly be moved from the terrace. She seemed to have forgotten everything in her rapt wonder at the place. She wanted to know what it was. What were all the people doing, where were they going, why did they go around bumping into each other and never speaking? If it was a railway station, where were the trains, and why was it so beautiful? What was the Zodiac, and why didn't one see it in the sky outside? It suddenly struck George as particularly strange that a girl who professed to come from Chillicothe, Ohio, should know nothing about the Grand Central Station.

"By the way," he said. "Didn't your train from Ohio come to this station?"

"Oh, dear no," she threw off carelessly. "I crossed the river on a ferry-boat." She had parried that. George piloted her as quickly as possible toward the waiting-room. He was very angry; he said to himself that he had never been the victim of such a flagrant fiction.

"Look here!" he said, as they sat side by side. "How long have you been in New York?"

"About two weeks – but I haven't seen half – "

"And I suppose you've tried to get a job everywhere," George sneered, "but there wasn't any work. And now you're turned out of your room, and they've seized your baggage!"

"O yes," nodded the girl, a little troubled. "They did all that. But you're mistaken. It wasn't that I couldn't get a job. I didn't try to find a job. You see, I've been riding on the Seeing-New-York automobiles all day long every day, and that costs a dollar a ride, and there are so many places they don't go."

George was mad. "O come," he said. "You can't expect me to believe that. I live here, you know. (George is very proud of being a New Yorker.) Perhaps if you'd tell me the truth, I could help you."

The girl gave a sudden surprised little chuckle, and bent her round eyes upon him.

"Why, mother always said I was a dreadful fibber. And maybe I made some things sound worse'n they really are. But I guess I know what you mean," she went on gently. "You think I've – that I – But no, no, no." She shook her head. "I know all about things but I'm a good girl."

George felt a sharp pain in his heart. He had hurt himself. As for the girl, she seemed to dismiss the incident from her mind. There was a pause.

"What are you going to do?" he asked finally, in a stiff voice.

"That's what I wanted to talk to you about." She turned to him a little excitedly. "You see, last night when I went home to my room she wouldn't let me in; and she said through a crack in the door that she wouldn't give me my clothes. So I walked around thinking what to do. It was so much fun going down the quiet streets in the night and the gray morning that I forgot to think much what I *was* going to do. And then I slept a little while at Macy's – and – and – Well, I'd just about made up my mind when I saw you."

"Well, what?" he asked impatiently.

"Well, I think I've got to see the rest of New York. Only I guess it'll cost money. You see, I've got to eat and sleep. Eat anyway." Here she puckered her brow in a delightful little frown. "And that's what I want to ask your advice about."

The simple-minded recklessness of this fairly took George off his feet. Always providing the story was not a deliberate lie. And, great Heavens, how he wanted to doubt that story!

"Look here!" he said. "You go home to Chillicothe. That's my advice. You go home. Why, you don't know the risks you run in this terrible city! (New Yorkers love their Sodom and Gomorrah.) You could starve to death as easily as not. And as for the other things – well, it's lucky you didn't meet some of the men that live in this town. Ugh! (George shuddered to think of some of the monsters that infest Babylon.) Suppose it hadn't been me. Do you know what any man would have thought?"

"Yes," she said unsmilingly. "Just what you thought. And he'd do pretty much what you're doing, too. I'm not afraid of men. I always trusted everybody, and nobody ever did me any harm. O, I've lived through a good deal, and being hungry doesn't scare me much. Somebody always helps me – and that's because I've got faith."

"You go home!" said George roughly. "You don't know what you're talking about! I'll get you a ticket and give you money enough to buy your food. Go home to your mother quick, before you get caught in the whirlpool. (George is pretty proud of his metaphors.) Now I know you don't want to go, and you're a brave girl; but if you don't I swear I'll – "

He was about to threaten her with the Gerry Society when he suddenly saw that her face was buried in her hands and her shoulders shaking. Was she laughing at him? He pulled her arm brutally away from her face. She seemed to be shaken with sobs, although there were no tears.

Poor George didn't know what to think.

"Oh!" she said brokenly. "You're right. I want to go home. I've been just going on my nerve. O send me home."

George asked her how much the fare was, and in the end it came to about twenty dollars, according to her. It also developed that a train left in fifteen minutes which would take her on her way.

"Now," said George. "Come on. We'll go and buy your ticket."

The girl had stopped crying with unnatural suddenness, George says, and not the slightest trace of it remained. At this remark she stood still and laid her grimy little hand on his arm.

"No," she said. "Give me the money and let me buy it myself." George looked sardonic. "You didn't believe me, and you must, or else I'll have to find someone else. Let's say good-by here."

George hesitated only a moment. Then he said to himself, "O well, what if she is stinging me? What if she does take my money and go out the Forty-second Street door? I'm a damn fool already, anyhow." And he gave her the money.

She must have seen what he was thinking. For she fixed her eyes steadily on his, shaking her head in that quaint way of hers.

"You've got no faith," she said. "But never mind. Because you're good to me I'll tell you where I lived in New York. And you can go there. . . ."

After she had gone, leaving him in the waiting-room, he came home and was indiscreet enough to tell us all about it. Of course we guyed him to death for a sentimental sucker, and he got pretty ashamed of his knight-errantry. The more so because he wasn't that kind of fellow at all.

At dinner Burgess argued the matter out with him.

"I know the kind," said Burgess loftily. "I suppose she kissed you purely just before you parted?"

"No," answered George. "And that was funny, because I wanted to. You'd have thought gratitude – "

"Well, then, she took your name and address and promised some day to pay it back!"

"On the contrary. She gave me hers – where she said all her baggage was held up. And I, when the reaction came on me, went up there, knowing that I wouldn't find anything."

"And you didn't?"

George shrugged. "It's all out here in the hall now. That suitcase. All – all just as she said."

"I'll frankly admit," said Burgess, "that I never heard of anything like it before. But the girl doesn't exist – or the man either – who would quit this town with twenty new dollars. No, sir. The explanation is that she strayed out of her district. Now that she's flush, she'll go back there. I'll bet, if you hunted long enough you could find her almost any night on Sixth Avenue near Thirty-third Street."

And they bet five on that, although I didn't see any sense in it.

One night about three weeks later, George came in and marched straight up to Burgess, saying, "Here's your five!"

"What for?" asked Burgess, who had forgotten as completely as any of us.

"Saw the girl," muttered George, without looking anybody in the eye. "Sixth Avenue and Thirty-third Street."

"Tell us," said Burgess, who was a real sport after all. And so we heard the sequel.

George had spent the holiday out on Long Island with the Winslows, and had taken the eight-ten train. He got in to the Pennsy Station about a quarter past nine and thought he'd walk down. And at the corner of Thirty-third and Sixth Avenue, who should bump into him but the girl! George says that he was paying no attention to anything but his own thoughts, when some one cried out to him:

"Going anywhere in particular?"

He looked up suddenly and recognized her. She passed him a few feet, and now turned squarely in the middle of the sidewalk and rested her hands on her hips like a small washerwoman. A little flurry of anger swept him – but it was a long time since the incident, and he decided to feel cynically amused.

"I'm going with you," he mimicked calmly, and joined her. "Where do you want to go?"

For answer she stepped up to him, took him by both shoulders, and looked into his face, shaking her head slowly back and forth.

"I want something to eat," is all she said, simply. George shrugged his shoulders and mentioned Baber's. That searching look of hers had made him most uncomfortable, and as they walked along he covertly glanced at her. It seemed to him that she was thinner, less well-nourished, smaller, shabbier – but just as innocent. That was another proof of her guilt. For no one could run around the streets for five weeks and remain undefiled. So she must have been always spotted. And her candid, untroubled expression as she walked beside him – when any ordinary girl would have begun at once to explain. (George is a rare analyst of human nature.)

"You know," she said, "it's lucky I met you. I haven't had anything to eat today."

"Why me particularly?" sneered George. "Won't the others stand for it?"

"O yes," she said quietly. "Somebody always takes me to lunch or something. But I just didn't feel hungry all day. I've been down on the docks looking at the ships. It's like a picture of the world there. Every ship smells of somewhere else." George decided to revenge himself upon her by not mentioning the matter of their former visit. If she possessed a conscience, that would punish her. "And oh," she remembered all at once. "You are my friend and I don't mind asking – I need ten dollars to pay for a suit I ordered; you see, I'm still wearing my old clothes, and they're not warm enough."

"Well!" gasped George. "Of all the nerve!"

"Well, perhaps it was pretty nervy to order it," assented the girl.

Alas for George's good resolutions. When the suspicious head-waiter at Baber's had been reassured by the whiteness of George's linen, the poor fellow's impatient curiosity consumed him bodily. What would she say? How would she explain it? Or would she simply own up to the fraud? Or would she tell as marvelous and incredible a story as before? The object of his conjectures was calmly looking around the room, contented, sufficient, aloof. He couldn't stand it any longer.

"I thought you went back to Chillicothe." George was very ironic. She glanced at him, and he thought he detected a faint gleam of amusement in her eyes, and a faint shadow of sadness.

"I forgot that you'd want to hear about that first," she said. "Well, when I left you, I got on the train" – she paused, searching his face, and then repeated – "I got on the train – and rode along as far as Albany. And after that a really nice man came and sat down beside me and we got to talking. He was a tall, red man, with a yellow mustache – lots older than you – and his name was Tom, he said. Now I was thinking to myself, 'Here you are going back home with only the clothes on your back, after your mother worked all winter to make you enough clothes for this one. You never ought to have left New York without getting your things out of that boarding-house.' And I was worrying about going back to Chillicothe without them, so I told Tom about it. He said, 'Come on and get off at Utica, and I'll take you back to New York and get your clothes out of the boarding-house for you.'"

"This beats the other story," said George.

"You see?" she answered radiantly. "I told you before that I just had to see the rest of New York. And there was Tom when I needed him. Well, we got back here and he did all he said he would. But when we got to the boarding-house, the clothes were gone. They told me a young man had taken them, and I knew right away it was you. But I didn't know where to find you," she continued, smiling at him, "unless I went and walked up and down in front of that place where I saw you first. And Tom didn't want me to do that. You see, Tom was awfully good to me. He got me a room and paid two weeks rent in advance; and he bought me some nice dresses. We used to go to dinner together every night."

"What became of Tom?" asked George, with just the proper cynical inflection.

Which, however, the girl didn't seem to notice, because she went on, in a softer voice, "Poor Tom. He didn't understand. I don't know why, but I don't think he *could* understand. I think he must have been sick, or something. Because, after he had been so good to me, all that time, he suddenly began to – O, well, you know what he wanted. Poor Tom!"

"O, this is rich," cried George, rocking.

She gazed at him meditatively. "I wonder if even you understand?" she asked. "It wasn't his fault – I know that. He was too nice to me to be so mean. He just didn't understand. But of course I couldn't stay there; and I couldn't go on wearing his dresses. So I walked out one night, and that was a week ago."

"Where are you living now?"

"Well, I haven't any room just now – "

"What!" burst from him in spite of himself. "A whole week? But – "

The girl smiled mysteriously – or perhaps it was maliciously. "When night comes," she said quietly, "I just pick out some nice-looking house and ring the doorbell. And I say to the people, I am tired and I have no place to go, and I want to sleep here."

"And – ?" asked George, playing the game.

"Well, it's only once in a while that they don't understand. Then I just have to go to another house."

George poked a finger at her across the table. "I don't know why I listen to your tales," he said in a hard voice. "But I guess it's because I think you must be all right at bottom. Come now, please tell me the absolute truth. I know it's hard for a girl to get a job; but have you really tried?"

"Tried to get a job? Me? Why, no!" she looked surprised. "I don't want to work here. I want to see things. And O, there are so many millions of things to see and feel! Yesterday I walked – a long distance I walked, from early in the morning until almost noon. I went up a long shining street that climbed the roofs of the houses, between enormous quivering steel spider webs, until at last I could look down on miles and miles of smoky city spread flat – where all the streets boiled over with children. Think of it! All that to see – and I didn't know it was there at all!"

George says he had the strangest, most irrational sensation – for a moment he actually believed the girl. He seemed to look into a world whose existence he had never dreamed of – a world from which he was eternally excluded, because he knew too much! It hurt. The girl might have been a little white flame burning him. And in his pain he had to say all this. But she just wagged her little head solemnly.

"No," she said. "It's because you know too little."

But of course this curious mood only lasted a second. Then his common sense came back, and he told her just what he thought of her, and left her.

But one of the queerest things about the whole business was her parting from him. He says that she listened to all he said with her head birdlike on one side, and when he had finished she leaned over and took one of his hands in both of hers, and pressed it against her breast. Then her eyes filled with tears, and just when he thought she was going to cry, she burst out laughing.

"We'll meet again," she cried shrilly. "I'll see you just when I need you most – "

And then the indignant George went home.

"Well," said Burgess, twisting the five-dollar bill over and over, when the story was done. "Well, it's such a good story that I'm willing to pay for hearing it. I'll stand five of that ten – "

"What ten?" snapped George.

"That ten you gave her to pay for her suit," and Burgess held out the bill.

George stood there, getting redder and redder, looking at all of us to see if we were laughing at him. Then he said "Thanks" in a stifled voice and took it.

1913

ANOTHER CASE OF INGRATITUDE

Walking late down Fifth Avenue, I saw him ahead of me, on the dim stretch of sidewalk between two arc-lights. It was biting cold. Head sunk between hunched-up shoulders, hands in his pockets, he shuffled along, never lifting his feet from the ground. Even as I watched him, he turned, as if in a daze, and leaned against the wall of a building, where it made an angle out of the wind. At first I thought it was shelter he sought, but as I drew nearer I discerned the unnatural stiffness of his legs, the way his cheek pressed against the cold stone, and the glimmer of light that played on his sunken, closed eyes. The man was asleep!

Asleep – the bitter wind searching his flimsy clothes and the holes in his shapeless shoes; upright against the hard wall, with his legs rigid as an epileptic's. There was something bestial in such gluttony of sleep.

I shook him by the shoulder. He slowly opened an eye, cringing as though he were often disturbed by rougher hands than mine, and gazed at me with hardly a trace of intelligence.

"What's the matter – sick?" I asked.

Faintly and dully he mumbled something, and at the

same time stepped out as if to move away. I asked him what he said, bending close to hear.

"No sleep for two nights," came the thick voice. "Nothing to eat for three days." He stood there obediently under the touch of my hand, swaying a little, staring vacantly at me with eyes that hung listlessly between opening and shutting.

"Well, come on," I said, "we'll go get something to eat and I'll fix you up with a bed." Docilely he followed me, stumbling along like a man in a dream, falling forward and then balancing himself with a step. From time to time his thick lips gave utterance to husky, irrelevant words and phrases. "Got to sleep walking around," he said again and again. "They keep moving me on."

I took his arm and guided him into the white door of an all-night lunch-room. I sat him at a table, where he dropped into a dead sleep. I set before him roast beef, and mashed potatoes, and two ham sandwiches, and a cup of coffee, and bread and butter, and a big piece of pie. And then I woke him up. He looked up at me with a dawning meaning in his expression. The look of humble gratitude, love, devotion was almost canine in its intensity. I felt a warm thrill of Christian brotherhood all through my veins. I sat back and watched him eat.

At first he went at it awkwardly, as if he had lost the habit. Mechanically he employed little tricks of table manners – perhaps his mother had taught them to him. He fumblingly changed knife and fork from right hand to left, and then put down his knife and took a dainty piece of bread in his left hand; removed the spoon from his coffee cup before he drank, and spread butter thinly and painstakingly on his bread. His motions were so somnambulistic that I had a strange feeling of looking on a previous incarnation of the man.

As the dinner progressed, a marvelous change took place. The warmth and nourishment, heating and feeding his thin blood, flooded the nerve centers of that starving body; a quick flush mounted to his cheeks, every part of him started widely awake, his eyes glowed. The little niceties of manner dropped away as if they had never been. He slopped his bread roughly in the gravy, and thrust huge knife-loads of food into his mouth. The coffee vanished in great gulps. He became an individual instead of a descendant; where there had been a beast, a spirit lived; he was a man!

The metamorphosis was so exciting that I could hardly wait to learn more about him. I held in, however, until he had finished his dinner.

As the last of the pie disappeared, I drew forth a box of cigarettes and placed them before him. He took one and accepted one of my matches. "T'anks!" he said.

"How much will it cost you for a bed – a quarter?" I asked.

"Yeh," he answered. "T'anks!"

He sat looking rather nervously at the table – inhaling great clouds of smoke. It was my opportunity.

"What's the matter – no work?"

He looked me in the eye, for the first time since dinner had begun, in a surprised manner. "Sure," he said briefly. I noticed, with somewhat of a shock, that his eyes were gray, whereas I had thought them brown.

"What's your job?"

He didn't answer for a moment. "Bricklayer," he grunted. What was the matter with the man?

"Where do you come from?"

Même jeu. "Albany."

"Been here long?"

"Say," said my guest, leaning over. "Wot do you t'ink I am, a phonygraft?"

For a moment I was speechless with surprise. "Why, I was only asking to make conversation," I said feebly.

"Naw, you wasn't. You t'ought just because you give

me a hand-out, I'd do a sob-story all over you. Wot right have you got to ask me all them questions? I know you fellers. Just because you got money you t'ink you can buy me with a meal. . . ."

"Nonsense!" I cried. "I do this perfectly unselfishly. What do you think I get out of feeding you?"

He lit another one of my cigarettes.

"You get all you want," he smiled. "Come on now, don't it make you feel good all over to save a poor starvin' bum's life? God! You're pure and holy for a week!"

"Well, you're a strange specimen," I said angrily. "I don't believe you've got a bit of gratitude in you."

"Gratitude Hell!" said he easily. "Wot for? I'm t'anking my luck, not you – see? It might as well 'a' been me as any other bum. But if you hadn't struck me, you'd 'a' hunted up another down-and-outer. You see," he leaned across the table, explaining, "you just had to save somebody tonight. I understand. I got an appetite like that, too. Only mine's women."

Whereupon I left that ungrateful bricklayer and went to wake up Drusilla, who alone understands me.

1913

MAC – AMERICAN

I met Mac down in Mexico – Chihuahua City – on New Year's Eve. He was a breath from home, an American in the raw. I remember that as we sallied out of the hotel for a Tom-and-Jerry at Chee Lee's the cracked bells in the ancient cathedral were ringing wildly for midnight mass. Above us were the hot desert stars. All over the city, from the *cuartels* where Villa's army was quartered, from the distant outposts on the naked hills, from the sentries in the streets, came the sound of exultant shots. A drunken officer passed us, and mistaking the *fiesta*, yelled "Christ is born!" At the next corner down a group of soldiers, wrapped to their eyes in *serapes*, sat around a fire chanting the interminable ballad called "Morning Song to Francisco Villa." Each singer had to make up a new verse about the exploits of the Great Captain. . . .

At the great doors of the church, through the shady paths of the Plaza, visible and vanishing again at the mouths of dark streets, the silent, sinister figures of black-robed women gathered to wash away their sins. And from the cathedral itself, a pale red light streamed out – and strange Indian voices singing a chant that I had heard only in Spain.

"Let's go in and see the service," I said. "It must be interesting."

"Hell, no!" said Mac, in a slightly strained voice. "I don't want to butt in on a man's religion."

"Are you a Catholic?"

"No," he replied. "I don't guess I'm anything. I haven't been in a church for years."

"Bully for you!" I cried. "So you're not superstitious, either!"

Mac looked at me with some distaste. "I'm not a religious man." He spat. "But I don't go around knocking God. There's too much risk in it."

"Risk of what?"

"Why, when you die – you know. . . ." Now he was disgusted and angry.

In Chee Lee's we met up with two more Americans. They were the kind that preface all remarks by "I've been in this country seven years, and I know the people down to the ground!"

"Mexican women," said one, "are the rottenest on earth. Why, they never wash more than twice a year. And as for Virtue – it simply doesn't exist! They don't get married even. They just take anybody they happen to like. Mexican women are all whores, that's all there is to it!"

"I got a nice little Indian girl down in Torreon," began the other man. "Say, it's a crime. Why, she don't even care if I marry her or not! I – "

"That's the way with 'em," broke in the other. "Loose! That's what they are. I've been in the country seven years."

"And do you know," the other man shook his finger severely at me. "You can tell all that to a Mexican Greaser and he'll just laugh at you! That's the kind of dirty skunks they are!"

"They've got no pride," said Mac, gloomily.

"Imagine," began the first compatriot. "Imagine what would happen if you said that to an *American*!"

Mac banged his fist on the table. "The American Woman, God bless her!" he said. "If any man dared to dirty the fair name of the American Woman to me, I think I'd kill him." He glared around the table, and as none of us besmirched the reputation of the Femininity of the Great Republic, he proceeded. "She is a Pure Ideal, and we've got to keep her so. I'd like to hear anybody talk rotten about a woman in my hearing!"

We drank our Tom-and-Jerries with the solemn righteousness of a Convention of Galahads.

"Say, Mac," the second man said abruptly. "Do you remember them two little girls you and I had in Kansas City that winter?"

"*Do* I?" glowed Mac. "And remember the awful fix you thought you were in?"

"Will I ever forget it!"

The first man spoke. "Well," he said, "you can crack up your pretty señoritas all you want to. But for *me,* give me a clean little American girl. . . ."

Mac was over six feet tall – a brute of a man, in the magnificent insolence of youth. He was only twenty-five, but he had seen many places and been many things: railroad foreman, plantation overseer in Georgia, boss mechanic in a Mexican mine, cow-puncher, and Texas deputy-sheriff. He came originally from Vermont. Along about the fourth Tom-and-Jerry, he lifted the veil of his past.

"When I came down to Burlington to work in the lumber mill, I was only a kid about sixteen. My brother had been working there already a year, and he took me up to board at the same house as him. He was four years older than me – a big guy, too; but a little soft. . . . Always kept bulling around about how wrong it was to fight, and that kind of stuff. Never would hit me – even when he got hot at me because he said I was smaller.

"Well, there was a girl in the house, that my brother

53

had been carrying on with for a long time. Now I've got the cussedest damn disposition," laughed Mac. "Always did have. Nothing would do me but I should get that girl away from my brother. Pretty soon I did it. Well, gentlemen, do you know what that devil of a girl did? One time when my brother was kissing her, she suddenly says, 'Why, you kiss just like Mac does!' . . .

"He came to find me. All his ideas about not fighting were gone, of course – not worth a damn with a real man.

He was so white around the gills that I hardly knew him – eyes shooting fire like a volcano. He says, 'damn you, what have you been doing with my girl?' He was a great big fellow, and for a minute I was a little scared. But then I remembered how soft he was, and I was game. 'If you can't hold her,' I says, 'leave her go!'

"It was a bad fight. He was out to kill me. I tried to kill him, too. A big, red cloud came over me, and I went raging, tearing mad. See this ear?" Mac indicated the stump of the member alluded to. "He did that. I got him in one eye, though, so he never saw again. We soon quit using fists; we scratched, and choked, and bit, and kicked. They say my brother let out a roar like a bull every few minutes, but I just opened my mouth and screamed all the time. . . . Pretty soon I landed a kick in – a place where it hurt, and he fell like he was dead. . . ." Mac finished his Tom-and-Jerry.

Somebody ordered another. Mac went on.

"A little while after that I came away South, and my brother joined the Northwest Mounted Police. You remember that Indian who murdered the fellow out in Victoria in 'o6? Well, my brother was sent out after him, and got shot in the lung. I happened to be up visiting the folks – only time I ever went back – when my brother came home to die. . . . But he got well. I remember the day I went away he was just out of bed. He walked to the station with me, begging me to speak just one word to him. He held out his hand for me to shake, but I just turned on him and says, 'You son of a bitch!' A little later he started back to the job but died on the way. . . ."

"Gar!" said the first man. "Northwestern Mounted Police! That must be a job. A good rifle and a good horse and no closed season on Indians! That's what I call Sport!"

"Speaking of Sport," said Mac, "the greatest sport in the world is hunting niggers. After I left Burlington, you remember, I drifted down South. I was out to see the world from top to bottom, and I had just found out I could scrap. God! The fights I used to get into. . . . Well, any-way, I landed up on a cotton plantation down in Georgia, near a place called Dixville; and they happened to be shy of an overseer, so I stuck.

"I remember the night perfectly, because I was sitting in my cabin writing home to my sister. She and I always hit it off, but we couldn't seem to get along with the rest of the family. Last year she got into a scrape with a drum-mer – and if I ever catch that – Well, as I say; I was sitting there writing by the light of a little oil lamp. It was a sticky, hot night, and the window screen was just a squirm-ing mass of bugs. It made me itch all over to see 'em crawl-ing around. All of a sudden, I pricked up my ears, and the hair began to stand right up on my head. It was dogs – blood hounds – coming licketty-split in the dark. I don't know whether you fellows ever heard a hound bay when he's after a human. . . . Any hound baying at night is about the lonesomest, *doomingest* sound in the world. But this was worse than that. It made you feel like you were stand-ing in the dark, waiting for somebody to strangle you to death – *and you couldn't get away!*

"For about a minute all I heard was the dogs, and then somebody, or some Thing, fell over my fence, and heavy feet running went right past my window, and a sound of breathing. You know how a stubborn horse breathes

55

when they're choking him around the neck with a rope? That way.

"I was out on my porch in one jump, just in time to see the dogs scramble over my fence. Then somebody I couldn't see yelled out, so hoarse he couldn't hardly speak, 'Where'd he go?'

"'Past the house and out back!' says I, and started to run. There was about twelve of us. I never did find out what that nigger did, and I guess most of the men didn't either. We didn't care. We ran like crazy men, through the cotton field, and the woods swampy from floods, swam the river, dove over fences, in a way that would tire out a man ordinarily in a hundred yards. And we never felt it. The spit kept dripping out of my mouth – that was the only thing that bothered me. It was full moon, and every once in a while when we came to an open place somebody would yell, 'There he goes!' and we'd think the dogs had made a mistake, and take after a shadow. Always the dogs ahead, baying like bells. Say, did you ever hear a bloodhound when he's after a human? It's like a bugle! I broke my shins on twenty fences, and I banged my head on all the trees in Georgia, but I never felt it. . . ."

Mac smacked his lips and drank.

"Of course," he said, "when we got up to him, the dogs had just about torn that coon to pieces."

He shook his head in shining reminiscence.

"Did you finish your letter to your sister?" I asked.

"Sure," said Mac, shortly. . . .

"I wouldn't like to live down here in Mexico," Mac volunteered. "The people haven't got any Heart. I like people to be friendly, like Americans."

1914

THE RIGHTS OF SMALL NATIONS

I was having my passport viséed in the Bulgarian consulate at Bucharest, when Frank came in on the same errand. I knew at once that he was an American. The tides of immigration had washed his blood, the Leyendecker brothers had influenced the cut of his nose and jaw, and his look and walk were direct and unsophisticated. He was blond, youthful, "clean-cut." Beneath the tweed imitation English clothes that Rumanian tailors affect, his body was the body of a college sprinter not yet gone soft, as economically built as a wild animal's.

As instinctively, too, as an animal, for he was not observant, he flair'd in me a kinsman, and said "Hello" with the superior inflection of one Anglo-Saxon greeting another in the presence of foreign and inferior peoples. He was a communicative boy, too long away from home to be suspicious of Americans. If I were going by the one-thirty train to Sofia, he said, we might travel together. He himself had been working for the Romano-Americano Oil Company – a subsidiary alias for Standard Oil – for two years, in the Rumanian petroleum-fields near Ploesti. And as we walked down the street together he said that he was going to England to enlist in the army and fight.

"What for?" I cried out in astonishment.

"Well," he said earnestly, looking at me with troubled eyes and shaking his head, "there's a bunch of Englishmen out at Ploesti, and they told me all about it. I don't care – perhaps it's foolish, like everybody says out in our camp – but I can't help it. I've got to go. I think it was a dirty trick to violate the neutrality of Belgium."

"The neutrality of Belgium!" said I, with a sense of awe at the preposterous possibilities of human nature.

"Yes," he rushed on, "it makes me hot to think of a little country like Belgium and a big bully of a country like Germany. It's a damn shame! England is fighting for the rights of small nations, and I don't see how anybody can keep out of it that's got any guts!"

Some hours later I saw him on the station platform, talking to a thin, plain girl in a yellow cotton dress, who wept and powdered her nose simultaneously. His face was flushed and frowning, and he spat out his words the way a strong man does when he's angry at his dog, his servant, or his wife. The girl wept monotonously; sometimes she touched him with a timid, hungry gesture, but he shook off her hand.

He caught sight of me and brusquely quitted her, coming over with a shamefaced expression. He was evidently worried and exasperated. "Be with you as soon as I get rid of this damn woman!" he said, brutally masculine. "They can't leave a man alone, can they?"

Lighting a cigarette, he swaggered back to where she stood staring fixedly out along the track, her handkerchief crammed in her mouth, making a desperate effort to control herself. She had on excessively high-heeled slippers, such as Rumanian street-walkers wore that year, and carried a leather wrist-bag; everything about her was shabby. Her young breasts were flat, starved, and her knotted hair thin and dull. I knew that only a very unattractive girl could fail to make a living in Bucharest, where they boast more prostitutes to the square male than any other city in the world.

Her eyes involuntarily leaped to his face; she began to shake. Frank dug into his pockets in a surly way, pulled out a roll of banknotes, and peeled off two. The girl stiffened, went white and rigid; her eyes blazed. His outstretched hand with the money was like a loaded gun. But suddenly the dull red crept up her cheek like pain, and she clutched the bills and burst into violent sobbing. After all, she had to live.

My compatriot threw me a comic, despairing look and glowered at her. "What do you want?" he growled in harsh, unpleasant Rumanian. "I don't owe you anything. What are you bawling for? Run along home now. Goodby." He gave her a little clumsy push. She took two or three steps and stopped, as if she had no power to move further. And some instinct or some memory gave him a flash of understanding. He put his hands on her shoulders suddenly, and kissed her on the mouth. "Good-by," said the girl brokenly, and she ran.

We rattled south over the flat, hot plain, past wretched villages of mud huts roofed with filthy straw, halting long at little stations where the docile gaunt peasants in ragged white linen gaped stupidly at the train. The rich hectic whiteness of Bucharest vanished abruptly out of a world where people starved in hopeless misery.

"I don't understand women," Frank was saying. "You can't get rid of 'em when you're finished. Now I had that girl for about nine months. I gave her a good home to live in and better food to eat than she ever got in her life, and money – why, she spent on dresses and hats and postage stamps about a hundred and fifty dollars. But do you think she had any gratitude? Not her. When I got sick of her she thought she had a mortgage on the place – said she wasn't going to go. I had to push her out. Then afterward she began to write me hard-luck letters – nothing but a game to get money out of me. Fall for it? Of course I didn't fall for it. I'm not so easy as that! This morning I ran into her when I came up to take the train, and I swear I couldn't shake that skirt all day. Crying – ugh!"

"Where did you get her?" I asked.

"Her? Oh, I just picked her up on the street in Ploesti. ... You bet she'd never been with another fellow! That's dangerous." He looked at me, and a vague uncomfortableness made him desirous of justifying himself. "You see, out in the oil-fields every fellow has his own house. And you've got to eat and get washing done and have a clean place to live, of course. So everybody gets a girl to cook, wash, take care of the house and live with him. It's hard to get one who suits you all around. I've tried three, and I know fellows who've had six or eight; take 'em in, try 'em, kick 'em out.

"Pay? Why, you don't pay 'em anything. First place they live with you; don't they? And then they've got a house and food, and you buy their clothes for them. Nothing doing in the salary line. They might beat it with the money. No, that's the way you keep 'em on their good behavior. If they don't do what they're told, you shut down on their clothes."

I wanted to know if any of these *ménages* lasted.

"Well," said Frank, "there's Jordan. He's got the most beautiful house in our camp; you ought to see that place. But of course he leads a pretty lonely life, because only the unmarried boys ever come to see him; sometimes a married man, but never with his wife. Jordan's been living with a girl for eleven years – a Rumanian girl he took just like we take ours – and of course nobody will have anything to do with him. He's the cleverest guy in the company, that man, but they can't promote him while he lives like that. A high official out here has got to be more or less of a social light, you know. So he's sat there for years

60

and seen man after man that isn't worth a quarter what he is, passed over his head."

"Why doesn't he marry her?"

"What!" said Frank, surprised. "That kind of a woman? After her living with him all that time? Nobody would associate with her. She's not decent."

"Doesn't it hurt *your* prospects to live with women?"

"Oh, us! No, that's different. Everybody thinks it's all right, so long as we don't go around with the girls in public. You see, we're young fellows. It's only when you get about thirty that you must get married. I'm twenty-five."

"Then in five years – "

He nodded his yellow head. "I'll begin to think about getting a wife. But that's purely a business proposition. There's no use marrying – of course a real man has to have a woman once in a while, I know that, but I mean there's no use tying yourself up – unless you can get something good out of it. I'm going to pick a good-looker, with no scandal about her and a social pull that will help me in my job. Down South there's plenty of girls like that. I don't need her money – I can make a pretty good salary in a couple of years; and, besides, if your wife has an income of her own she's liable to want to do what she pleases. Don't you think so?"

"I think that's a rotten way to look at it," said I with heat. "If I lived with a girl, whether we were married or not, I'd make her my equal, financially and every other way." Frank laughed. "And as for your plans for marriage, how can you marry any one you don't love?"

"Oh, love!" Frank shrugged his shoulders with annoyance and looked out of the window. "Hell, if you're going to get sentimental. . . ."

1915

BROADWAY NIGHT

He stood on the corner of Broadway and Forty-second Street, a neat man with grayish side-whiskers, a placid mouth, benevolent spectacles perched on the tip of his nose, and the general air of a clergyman opposed to Preparedness on humane grounds. But on the front of his high-crowned derby hat was affixed a sheet labeled *Matrimonial News;* another hung down his chest, a third from his outstretched right arm, and he carried a pile of them on his left hand. And every little while his mouth fell mechanically open, and he intoned, in ministerial accents:

"Buy the *Matrimonial News.* If you want a wife or husband. Five cents a copy. Only a nickel for wedded bliss. Only half a dime for a lifetime of happiness."

He said this without any expression whatever, beaming mildly on the passing throng.

Floods of light – white, green, brazen yellow, garish red – beat upon him. Over his head a nine-foot kitten played with a monstrous spool of red thread. A gigantic eagle slowly flapped its wings. Gargantuan toothbrushes appeared like solemn portents in the sky. A green and red and blue and yellow Scotchman, tall as a house, danced a

62

silent hornpipe. Two giants in underclothes boxed with gloves a yard across. Sparkling beer poured from bottles into glasses topped with incandescent foam. Invisible fingers traced household words across the inky sky in letters of fire. And all between was ripples and whorls of colored flame.

"If you want a wife or husband. Only a nickel for wedded bliss," came the brassy voice.

He stood immovable, like a rock in a torrent. The theaters were just letting out. As a dynamited log-jam moves down the river, a double stream of smoking, screaming motors filled Broadway, Seventh Avenue, Forty-second Street, rushing, halting, breaking free again. . . . An illuminated serpent of street-cars blocked, clang-clanged.

The sidewalks ran like Spring ice going out, grinding and hurried and packed close from bank to bank. Ferret-faced slim men, white-faced slim women, gleam of white shirt-fronts, silk hats, nodding flowery broad hats, silver veils over dark hair, hard little somber hats with a dab of vermilion, satin slippers, petticoat-edges, patent-leathers, rouge and enamel and patches. Voluptuous exciting perfumes. Whiffs of cigarette smoke caught up to gold radiance, bluely. Café and restaurant music scarcely heard, rhythmical. Lights, sound, swift feverish pleasure. . . . First the flood came slowly, then full tide – furs richer than in Russia, silks than in the Orient, jewels than in Paris, faces, eyes and bodies the desire of the world – then the rapid ebb, and the street-walkers.

"Five cents a copy. Only half a dime for a lifetime of happiness."

"Can you guarantee it?" said I.

He turned upon me his calm and kindly gaze and took my nickel before answering.

"Turn to page two," he bade me. "See that photo? Read. 'Beautiful young woman, twenty-eight years old, in perfect health, heiress to five hundred thousand dollars, desires correspondence with bachelor; object matrimony, if right party can be found.' Thousands have achieved felicity through these pages. If you are disappointed," – he peered gravely over his glasses – "if you are disappointed, we give your nickel back."

"Have you tried it yourself?"

"No," he answered thoughtfully. "I will be frank with you. I have not." Here he interrupted himself to adjure the passing world: "Buy the *Matrimonial News*. If you want a wife or husband. . . .

"I have not," he went on. "I am fifty-two years old, and my wife is dead this day five years ago. I have known all of life; so why should I try?"

"Nonsense!" I exclaimed. "Nowadays life is not finished at fifty-two. Look at Walt Whitman and Susan B. Anthony."

"I am not acquainted with the parties you mention," responded the Matrimonial Newsboy seriously. "But I tell you, young man, the time of the end of living depends upon whether or not you have lived. Now I have lived." Here he turned from me to bawl "Five cents a copy. Only a nickel for wedded bliss. . . .

"My parents were working people. My father was killed by a fly-wheel in the pump-house of the Central Park Reservoir. My mother died of consumption brought on by doing piece-work at home. I was errand-boy in a haberdashery shop, bell-boy in a hotel, and then I drove a delivery-wagon for the *Evening Journal* until I was thrashed in a fight – my constitution was poorly – and so I went to Night School and became a clerk. I worked in several offices until finally I entered the Smith-Tellfair Company, Bankers and Brokers, 6 Broad Street. And there my life began." Methodical, unhurried, he again shouted the virtues of the *Matrimonial News*.

"At the age of twenty-seven, I fell in love, for the first

time in my life; and in time we married. I shall not dwell upon our initial hardships, nor the birth of our first child, who soon after died – largely because our means did not permit us to dwell in a neighborhood where there was sufficient light and air for a sickly baby.

"Afterward, however, things became more easy. I rose to be Chief Clerk at Smith-Tellfair's. By the time the second child was born – a girl – we had taken a small house at White Plains, for which I was gradually paying by the strictest economy in our living." Here he paused. "I have often wondered, after my experience, if thrift is really worth while. We might have had more pleasures in our life, and it would have all come to the same in the end." He seemed lost in meditation. Above, the nervous chaos of lights leaped in glory. Two women with white, high-heeled shoes passed, looking back over their shoulders at the furtive men. My friend called his wares once more.

"However. My little girl grew up. We had decided that she should learn the piano, and some day be a great musician with her name on an electric sign here." He waved his arm at Broadway. "When she was five years old, a son was born to me. He was to be a soldier – a general in the Army. When she was six years old, she died. The trouble was in the Town sewer-pipes – the contractors who did the work were corrupt, and so there was an epidemic of typhoid.

"She died, I say – Myrtle did. After that my wife was never quite the same. Unfortunately soon afterward she was going to have another baby. We knew that her condition wouldn't permit it, and tried our best to find some means of prevention. I've heard there were things – but we did not know them, and the doctor would do nothing. The child was born dead. My wife did not survive it.

"That left me and little Herbert – who was to be a general, you remember. It was about this time that young Mr. Tellfair succeeded his father at the head of the business; he was just out of college, with ideas about efficiency and office reorganization. And he discharged me first, for my hair was already white. . . . I then persuaded the Building and Loan Association to suspend my payments on the house for six months, while I procured another situation. Herbert was fourteen. It was extremely important that he remain in school, in order to prepare for the West Point examinations – for there he was to go.

"It was impossible for me to find another place as clerk, though I searched the city everywhere. I finally became night watchman in a paint and leather house near the financial district.

"Of course the salary was less than half what I had been earning. My payments on the house resumed, but I was unable to meet them. So I lost it.

"I brought Herbert with me to the city. He went to the Public School. And when he was sixteen, just twelve months ago, my little Herbert died of scarlet fever. Shortly afterward I stumbled upon this employment, which yields a comfortable living."

He ceased, and turning again to the passers-by, mildly called upon them to "Buy the *Matrimonial News*. Only a nickel for wedded bliss. Half a dime for a lifetime of felicity. . . ."

The glaring names, the vast excited conflagrations, the incandescent legs of kicking girls – all the lights that bedeck the façades of theaters – went out one by one. The imitation jewelry shops switched off their show-window illuminations; for wives and fiancées had gone home, and kept women, actresses and great *cocottes* were tangoing to champagne in dazzling cabarets. Domestic Science and Personal Hygiene still rioted across the sky. But Broadway was dimmer, quieter; and the fantastic girls parading by ones, by twos, with alert, ranging eyes, moved alluringly from light to shadow. In the obscurity men lurked, and around corners. They went along the street, with coat-collars pulled up and hats pulled down, devouring the women with hard eyes; their mouths were dry, and they shivered with fever and the excitement of the chase.

"Here. Gimme one," said a voice like rusty iron. A fat woman in a wide, short skirt, high-heeled gray shoes laced up the back, a pink hat the size of a button, held out a nickel in pudgy fingers gloved in dirty white. From behind, at a distance of three blocks in a dark street, you might have thought her young. But close at hand her hair had silver threads among the bleached, and there were white dead lumps of flesh under all that artifical red – hollows and wrinkles.

"Good evening, madam," said my friend, with a courtly lift of his hat. "I trust I find you well. How is business tonight?"

"It ain't what it used to be when I first done Broadway," responded the lady, shaking her head. "Pikers and charity boys nowadays – that's what it is. A couple of fresh guys got funny down by Shanley's – asked me to supper. God, what do you know about that? They was kidding me, it toined out. I been as swell places in my time as any goil in town. The idea! I met a fella up on Forty-fifth Street, and he says, 'Where'll we go?' And I says, 'I know a place over on Seventh Avenoo.' 'Seventh!' says he. 'Seven's my unlucky number. Good *night!*' and he beat it. The idea!" She shook with good-natured mirth. Presently I entered her horizon. "Who's your young friend, Bill?" said she. "Interdooce us." She dropped her voice: "Say, honey, want some fun? No?" She yawned, revealing gold teeth. "O well, it's time for bed anyhow. I'll go home and pound my ear off."

"Looking for a husband?" I asked, pointing to the *Matrimonial News.*

"The idea! Say, did you ever know a goil that wasn't?

If you got any nice friend with a million dollars, you leave word with Bill here. He sees me every night."

"But you only buy the *Matrimonial News* Saturday nights," said Bill.

"To read Sundays," she replied. "I get a real rest Sundays. I don't do no business on the Lord's day – never have." She proudly tossed her head. "Never have, no matter how broke I was. I was brought up strict, and I got religious scruples. . . ." She was gone, swaying her enormous hips.

The *Matrimonial News* agent folded up his papers.

"It's bed for me too, young man," said he, "so good night. As for you, I suppose you'll go helling about with drink and women." He nodded half sadly. "Well, go your ways. I'm past blaming anyone for anything."

I wandered down the feverish street, checkered with light and shade, crowned with necklaces and pendants and lavalliers and sunbursts of light, littered with rags and papers, torn up for subway construction, patrolled by the pickets of womankind. One tall, thin girl who walked ahead of me I watched. Her face was deadly pale, and her lips like blood. Three times I saw her speak to men – three times edge into their paths, and with a hawk-like tilt of her head murmur to them from the corner of her mouth.

I quickened my pace and passed her, and as I drew abreast she looked at me, coldly, a fierce invitation.

"Hello!" said I, slowing down. But she stopped suddenly, stared at me hatefully, a stranger, and drew herself up.

"To whom do you think you're talking to!" she asked, in a harsh voice. . . .

"This," said I, "is what they call Natural Selection!"

The next one was not so difficult. Around the corner

on Thirty-seventh Street she stood, and seemed to be waiting for me. We came together like magnet and steel, and clasped hands.

"Let's go somewheres and get a drink," said she.

She was robust and young, eager, red and black to look at. No one could dance like her, in the restaurant we went to. Every one turned to watch her – the blank-faced, insolent waiters, the flat-chested men biting cigars, the gay and discontented women who sat there as if it had all been created to set them off. In her black straw hat with the blue feather, her slightly shabby brown tweed suit, she blew into the soft warmth, gold, mirrors, hysterical ragtime of the place like a lawless wind.

We sat against the wall, watching the flush of faces, the whiteness of slim shoulders, hearing the too loud laughter, smelling cigarette smoke and the odor that is like the taste of too much champagne. Two orchestras brayed, drummed and banged alternately. A dance for the guests – then professional dancers and singers, hitching spasmodically, bawling flatly meaningless words to swift rhythm. Then the lights went out, all except the spot on the performers, and in the drunken dark we kissed hotly. Flash! Lights on again, burst of hard hilarity, whirl of shouting words, words, words, rush of partners to the dance floor, orchestra crashing syncopated breathless idiocy, bodies swaying and jerking in wild unison. . . .

Her name was Mae; she wrote it with her address and telephone number on a card, and gave references to South African diplomats who had enjoyed her charms, if I wanted recommendations. . . . Mae never read the newspapers, and was only vaguely conscious that there was a war. Yet how she knew Broadway between Thirty-third and Fiftieth streets! How perfectly she was mistress of her world!

She came from Galveston, Texas, she said – boasted that her mother was a Spaniard, and then hesitatingly admitted that her father was a gipsy. She was ashamed of that, and hardly ever told any one.

"But he wasn't one of these here gipsies that go like tramps along the road and steal things," added Mae, asserting the respectability of her parentage. "No. He come of a very fine gipsy family...."

1916

ENDYMION: *OR* ON THE BORDER

Presidio, Texas, is a collection of a dozen adobe shacks and a two-story frame store, scattered in the brush in the desolate sand-flat along the Rio Grande. Northward the desert goes rolling gently up against the fierce, quivering blue, a blasted and silent land. The flat brown river writhes among its sand-bars like a lazy snake, not a hundred yards away. Across the river the Mexican town of Ojinaga tops its little *mesa* – a cluster of white walls, flat roofs, the cupolas of its ancient church – an Oriental town without a minaret. South of that the terrible waste flings out in great uptilted planes of sand, mesquite and sage brush, crumpling at last into a surf of low sharp peaks on the horizon.

In Ojinaga lay the wreck of the Federalista army, driven out of Chihuahua by the victorious advance of Pancho Villa, and apathetically awaiting his coming here, by the friendly border. Thousands of civilians, scourged on by savage legends of the Tiger of the North, had accompanied the retreating soldiers across that ghastly four hundred miles of burning plain. Most of the refugees lay camped in the brush around Presidio, happily destitute, subsisting on the Commissary of the American Cavalry stationed here; sleeping all day, and singing, love-making and fighting all night.

The fortunes of war had thrust greatness upon Presidio. It figured in the news dispatches telephoned to the outer world by way of the single Army wire. Automobiles, gray with desert dust, roared down over the packtrail from the railroad, seventy-five miles north, to corrupt its pristine innocence. A handful of war-correspondents sat there in the sand, cursing, and twice a day concocted two-hundred-word stories full of sound and fury. Wealthy *hacendados,* fleeing across the border, paused there to await the battle which should decide the fate of their property. Secret agents of the Constitutionalistas and the Federal plotted and counterplotted all over the place. Representatives of big American interests distributed retaining fees, and sent incessant telegrams in code. Drummers for munition companies offered to supply arms wholesale and retail to anyone engaged in or planning a revolution. Not to mention – as they put it in musical comedy programs – citizens, Rangers, deputy Sheriffs, United States troopers, Huertista officers on furlough, Customs officials, cow-punchers from nearby ranches, miners, etc.

Old Schiller, the German store-keeper, went bellowing around with a large revolver strapped to his waist. Schiller was growing rich. He supplied food and clothing and tools and medicines to the swollen population; he had a monopoly on the freighting business; he was rumored to conduct a poker game and private bar in the back room; and sixty men slept on the floor and counters of his store for twenty-five cents a head.

I went around with a bow-legged, freckle-faced cowboy named Buchanan, who had been working on a ranch down by Santa Rosalia, and was waiting for things to clear up so he could go back. Buck had been three years in Mexico, but I couldn't discover it had left any impression on his mind – except a grievance against Mexicans for not speaking English; all his Spanish being a few words to satisfy his natural appetites. But he occasionally mentioned Dayton, Ohio – from which city he had fled on a freight-train at the age of twelve.

He seemed to be a common enough type down there; a strong, lusty body, brave, hard, untroubled by any spark of fine feeling. But I hadn't been with him many hours before he began to talk of Doc. According to Buck, Doc was Presidio's first citizen; he was a great surgeon, and more than that, one of the world's best musicians. But more remarkable than everything, to me, was the pride and affection in Buck's voice when he told of his friend.

"He kin set a busted laig with a grease-wood twig and a horse-hair riata," said Buck, earnestly. "And curing up a t'rant'ler bite ain't no more to him than taking a drink is to you or me. . . . And play – say! Doc kin play any kind of a thing. By God. I guess if anybody from New York or Cleveland was to hear him tickle them instruments, he would be a-setting on the Opera House stage right now, instead of the sand at Presidio!"

I was interested.

"Doc who?" I asked.

Buck looked surprised. "Why, just Doc," he said.

After supper that night I plowed through the sand in the direction of Doc's adobe cabin. It was a still night, with great stars. From somewhere up the river floated down the sound of a few lazy shots. All around in the brush flared the fires of the refugee camps; women screamed nasally to their children to come home; girls laughed out in the darkness; men with spurs "kajunked" past in the sand; and like an accompaniment in the bass sounded the insistent mutter of a score of secret agents conspiring on the porch of Schiller's store. Long before I came near, I could hear the familiar strains of the *Tannhäuser* overture played on a castrated melodeon; and immediately in front of the house, I almost stumbled over a double row of Mexicans, squatting in the sand, wrapped to the eyes in *serapes,* rigidly listening.

Within the one white-washed room, two U. S. cavalry officers sat with their eyes closed, pretending to enjoy what they considered "high-brow" entertainment. They had been eight months on the Border, far from the refinements of civilization, and it made them feel "cultured" to hear that kind of music. Buchanan, smoking a corn-cob pipe, lay stretched in an armchair, his feet on the stove, his glistening eyes fixed with frank enjoyment on Doc's fingers as they hopped over the keys. Doc himself sat with his back to us – a pathetic, pudgy, white-haired little figure. Some of the melodeon keys produced no sound at all; others a faint wheeze; and the rest were out of tune. As he played he sang huskily, and swayed back and forth as one rapt in harmony.

It was a remarkable room. At one end stood the wreck of an elaborate glass-topped operating-table. Behind it, a case of rusty surgical instruments – the top shelf full of pill bottles – and a book-case containing five volumes: a book of Operatic Selections scored for the piano, part of a volume of Beethoven's Symphonies arranged for four hands, two volumes on Practical Diagnosis, and The Poems of John Keats, morocco-bound, hand-tooled, and worn. There was a desk, too, piled with papers. And all around the rest of the room were musical instruments in various stages of desuetude: concertina, violin, guitar, French horn, cornet, harp. A small Mexican hairless dog with a cataract in one eye, sat at Doc's feet, his nose lifted to the ceiling, howling continuously.

Doc played more and more furiously, humming as his gnarled fingers jumped about over the keyboard. Suddenly, in the midst of a thundering chord, he stopped, turned half around to us and stretching out his hands, mumbled through his whiskers:

"M' hands are too small! Every damn thing's wrong

about me somewhere. Aye!" He sighed. "Franz Liszt had short fingers, too. Hee! Not like mine. No short fingers in the head . . ." his words ran off into indistinguishable mumbling.

Buck brought his feet down with a crash, and slapped his knee.

"God, Doc!" he cried. "If you had big hands I don't know what in hell you couldn't do!"

Doc looked dully at the floor. The little dog put his feet upon his lap and whimpered, and the old man laid a trembling hand on his head. The two officers awkwardly took their leave. Presently Doc lit up a great pipe, grumbling and groaning to himself, the smoke oozing out of his mustache, nose, eyes and ears.

With a sort of reverence Buck introduced me. Doc nodded, and looked at me with bleary little eyes that didn't seem to see. His round, puffy face was covered with a white stubble; through a yellow, ragged mustache came indistinctly the ruins of a cultivated articulation. He smelt strongly of brandy.

"Aye – you're not one of these – sand-fleas umble-umble-umble," he said, blinking up at me. "From the great world. From the great world. Tell 'em my name is writ in water umble-umble."

No one knew anything about him except what he had dropped when drunk. He himself seemed to have forgotten his past. The Mexicans, among whom most of his practice was, loved him devotedly, and showed it by paying their bills. He always made the same charge for any medical service – setting a fracture, amputating a limb, delivering a child, or giving a dose of cough syrup – twenty-five cents. But he had spoken of London, Queen's Hall, the Conservatory of Music, and of being in India and Egypt, and of coming to Galveston as head of a hospital. Beyond that, nothing but the names of Mexican cities, of unknown people. All that Presidio knew of him was that he had come across the border nameless and drunk during the Madero revolution, and had stayed there nameless and drunk ever since.

"On the Maidan!" said Doc suddenly. "Riding in their carriages! And I – here. . . ." He rumbled on for a while, and hiccoughed. "Yes, it killed her, but I wasn't – "

I sat talking with him, trying to strike upon some key that would unlock his life.

"I hear you have been connected with the London Conservatory of Music."

He leaped to his feet, clenching both fists, and glared around. "Who said that?" he roared. Then he sat down again. "And now I am an old tramp doctor in Presidio!" he finished, and chuckled without bitterness.

I tried him with Egypt, and he said, "In those days there was a forest of masts in Alexandria roadstead – thick. . . ." Then I spoke of India, but he only muttered, "In Darjelling – at the big deodar on the lawn. Oh God . . . umble-umble. . . ."

"Galveston!" he cried, and straightened up. "Yes I was in Galveston when the flood – My wife was drowned. . . ." He said this without much feeling, and rising, went unsteadily to the book-case and took down one of the Practical Diagnosis books, which he brought back to me as a child might have done. On the flyleaf was the date *Galveston, September 18, 1901,* and newspaper clippings about the flood were stuck crazily underneath. I took it back to the book-case, and carelessly picking up the Poems of John Keats, opened it. Inside the cover was written, in ink that had almost faded:

June, 1878
To Endymion
With my body and soul
A. deH. K.

Endymion – he! To what woman was that battered old wreck ever Endymion? 1878. In his middle twenties, perhaps – beautiful, a dreamer.

I heard a sort of moaning snarl, and looked up to see Doc upon his feet, bent over and peering at me strangely.

"What have you got? What have you got?" he almost screamed. "Put it down...." As he came lurching at me I slipped the book back in the case. He grasped my two hands and lifted them up to his eyes, then dropped them and turned.

"Nothing," he mumbled. "I had forgotten.... I lost it in Monterey...." He stood still, muttering to himself. "Now what brought her back – drowned for thirty years? Well, drown her all over again!" He went to the corner and got a black bottle and tilted it to his lips. Then he reached down among his instruments and pulled out an old accordion, and sitting down in his chair again, began suddenly to play what could be recognized as Beethoven's Third Symphony. It was startling.

But he played only a minute; stopped, shook his head and sighed. "Eroica!" he said. "Eroica! Umble-umble-umble. What do you sand-fleas know about high tragedy? I'm getting old and I've hunted all my life and never found – " Found what? Fame? Wealth? Love? *Truth?* ...

The next evening we had supper, Buchanan, Doc and I, in a one-room Mexican restaurant, whose proprietor had once owned a little ranch across the river, which Enrique Creel had sold to William Randolph Hearst, pocketing the proceeds. As big, brown men, booted and spurred, came in, each one stopped at the head of the table to say "Howdye Doc! How ya coming?" The Mexican waiter served Doc first, and when a rich cattleman who had motored in that morning began cursing him for a lazy Greaser, one of the Rangers leaned over and tapped him on the arm.

"Doc gets his first, stranger," he said quietly. "After that you kin put *your* foot in the trough."

Doc had risen late, tormented by the fires of hell; and though he had already gulped down about a quart of *aguardiente,* it hadn't yet taken effect. He was black and silent, answering the greetings with a grunt.

Next to me sat a brisk little man with a retreating chin, a denizen of cities. He was agent for the Crayon Enlargement Home Portrait Company, of Kansas City, Mo., and was greatly pleased with the amount of business he had done in Presidio, taking pictures and getting orders from the Mexicans. The table sat listening to his piping little boasts with grave faces and insides full of mirth. As Buck explained to me afterward, a Mexican loves to get his picture taken; and a Mexican will order anything, or sign his name to anything – but he won't pay for it.

"Mexicans are fine subjects for photography," the agent was saying, enthusiastically. "They will hold a pose for fifteen minutes without moving – "

Doc suddenly lifted his head, rumbled a little and said distinctly:

"That is why I didn't have mine finished. It was hard work to pose for Freddie Watts umble-umble-umble."

"You mean in London?" I asked quickly.

"Hampst'd," answered Doc, absently. "His studio was in Hampst'd. . . ."

So if Doc hadn't been tired of posing, his portrait might be hanging with those of William Morris, Rossetti, George Meredith, Swinburne, Browning, in the National Gallery!

"Did you know William Morris?" I said, breathlessly.

"A damned prig!" shouted Doc suddenly, beating his fist on the table. Eagerly I asked him about the others; but he went on eating, as if he didn't hear. "Dilettantes – an age of petty amateurs!" he cried finally, and would say no more.

The Crayon Enlargement agent tapped his head to the

company and jerked a thumb at Doc. "Non-compos, ain't he?" he remarked with a knowing grin. "Bats in his attic, hey?" A prolonged hostile stare met his eyes. Down at the foot of the table a taciturn cowboy pointed a piece of bread at him, and remarked briefly:

"You wooden-headed *cabrito,* you better close up. Doc here's a friend of mine, and he's forgot more'n you'll ever know."

Doc never seemed to notice. But as we went outside afterward I heard him mutter something about "sand-fleas." We walked over toward a little shack where a pool-table had been set up, and I tried to find out just when he had dropped out of "the great world." He responded to the name of Pasteur, but Ehrlich, Freud and the other modern medical names I knew evidently meant nothing to him. In music, Saint-Saëns was evidently an interesting youngster and no more; Strauss, Debussy, Schönberg, even Rimski-Korsakov, were Greek to him. Brahms he hated, for some reason.

There was a game on in the pool-room when we came in, but some one set up a shout "Here comes Doc!" and the players laid down their cues. Doc and Buchanan played on the rickety table, while I sat by. The old man's game was magnificent; he never seemed to miss a shot, no matter how difficult, though he could hardly see the balls. Buck hardly got a chance to shoot. Around the walls on the ground sat a solid belt of Mexicans in high wide sombreros, with *serapes* of magnificent faded colors, great boot buckles and spurs as big as dollars. When Doc made a good shot a chorus of soft applause came from them. When he fumbled and dropped his pipe, ten hands scrambled for the honor of retrieving it. . . .

In the soft, deep, velvety night we started home through the sand. We had gone a little distance when Doc suddenly stopped.

"Here, Tobey! Here, Tobey!" he cried, swaying and

peering around in the dark. "I've lost my little dog. I wonder where that little dog is? I guess he must be back at the pool hall. Here, Tobey! I've got to go back and find my little dog."

"Hell, Doc," said Buck impatiently, "your dog'll come back. Let me go and get him for you. You're tired."

Doc shook his head, mumbling. "I've got to find my little dog," he said, "nobody can find – anything for me. Each has got to seek – alone umble-umble," and he turned back.

Buck and I squatted down by the trail and lit cigarettes. Around us the thick, exotic night was rich with sounds and smells. Buck abruptly began to speak:

"I don't remember nothing about my father," he said, "except he was a son of a bitch. But I thought all old men was like him; in fact, I never met a real man or any other kind of man who wasn't out for himself, until I run across Doc. All this Christian bunk never was nothing to me until now. But this Doc, he's got a kind of combination of awful goodness and just suffering like hell all the time that – well, I don't know, but I – I – love that man. And great – he's a great man I know that. He's big all through. Some damn fools around here say he's crazy; but I sometimes think all the rest of us is. He's drunk all the time, Doc is, but everything he says, even the wildest things, somehow hit me way deep down like God's truth."

Buck stopped, and we saw the chunky little figure of Doc loom up staggering in the dark, with Tobey trotting at his heels. We got up silently and walked along, one on each side of him. He didn't seem to notice us, mumbling and hiccoughing to himself. But suddenly he heaved a tremendous sigh, threw out both arms, and with his poor dim eyes on the sky, said:

"Heigh-ho! Night for the Gentiles is day-time for the Children of Israel!"

1916

JOHN BULL
IN AMERICA

THE THING TO DO

I came from the Pacific coast on the Lucullus Limited, which is, as you know, the boast of a great railroad system, the toy of a powerful board of directors – a train which loses an immense sum of money every trip it makes. For it provides all the comforts of a hotel and a club – a barber shop, bath, stenographer, vacuum cleaners, free newspapers, *and* tea in the observation car. About four-thirty a company of dignified colored waiters bear aft the ceremonial pots and cups, and ask some frightened cattle-king's wife to pour for a perfectly strange company. Then ensues a division of the classes. The cattle-king's wife emits a startled "How?" and flees; her husband, who has been snoring in his shirt-sleeves, with the children plucking at his elastic arm-bands, awakes, struggles frantically into his coat, and herds his progeny toward the smoking-room. By this time the polite waiters have hit upon the president of the Ladies' Club of Willow City, Wyoming, who nervously rises to the occasion. Directing her gaze haphazard upon the cow-puncher in his store-clothes who sits in the corner, she shouts "Cream or lemon?" Vainly he strives to answer; a dark flush mantles his brow as he says: "I guess I don't care for none!" Indignantly, the refined and genteel rush to the rescue; it is a pleasure to watch them flourish the implements of their social rite, with that ostentatious grace which is a rebuke to the uninitiate. Drawn together by the bond of superior civilization, the tea-drinkers are soon chatting with as little effort or intelligence as if they were in their own drawing-rooms; and from that moment, class-lines are sharply drawn, and no one who has flunked the ordeal may consort with any but his kind.

I first noticed the Englishman upon this occasion. Normally, few men braved the tea, for we Americans are an uncivilized breed, afraid of ridicule; the farther West you go, the more timid people are. However, when the dreadful preliminaries were over this afternoon, and a retired Army Wife had accepted the responsibility, the Englishman put down the magazine he was reading and looked boredly expectant. He was a clean-cut young man, with nice color, a neat mustache, clothes that fitted exquisitely, and shoes too large – typical, unobjectionable, correct.

The Army Wife appealed to him with her eyes.

"One or two lumps? Cream – ?"

Cattle-kings, wheat-barons, their wives, their children, cowboys, drummers, focused their gaze upon the Englishman, their mouths hanging open so as to catch every word. They were most curious to know what a man should answer under such circumstances.

"Thanks," said the Englishman, without a shade of expression in voice or face. "One lump. Cream, if you please."

From the audience came a sound of relief, of admiration. Breath was expelled. A few children snickered in a frightened way. The common herd began to feel a little *de trop,* but they lingered in their going to see what the Englishman would do with his tea when he got it. After that, they faded away up the corridor or out onto the observation platform, leaving the place to the elect, who, thanks to the Englishman's example, now numbered eight or more.

The Army Wife said afterward how nice he had been. I'm sure he had no idea of being nice. No, he had taken tea because it was a part of the immutable law of his universe. . . .

I saw him several times after that. He spoke to hardly any one – he seemed not to need companionship like the rest of us. It wasn't that he didn't know how, or that he felt socially superior – he was simply satisfied with himself perfectly and entirely. He read seldom. He didn't have to read. He sat in a chair in the smoking compartment for hours at a time, smoking a pipe – and ruminating.

As I passed him in the corridor or walking up and down station platforms when we stopped for a minute, he would remove the pipe from his mouth, shake his head diagonally, smile briefly, and ejaculate "*Good* morning." After two or three days I even surprised him in conversation with the Army Wife, whom he could talk to because he had met her socially.

"What does he talk about?" I asked her curiously.

"Oh, cricket and Switzerland," she cried, ecstatically. "He was once in Switzerland. But I simply love to hear him pronounce his words. And he is so restful. You know exactly what he'll say next!"

I was surprised at his talking of Switzerland, because it is not good taste for an Englishman to mention places where he has been. Nor people he knows; nor anything that smacks of theory. Indeed, there is very little a cultivated Englishman can discuss with a stranger, and not lose dignity, except the weather.

But in the smoking compartment, especially the smoking compartment of such a train as the Lucullus Limited, an Anglo-Saxon will sometimes unbend so far as to deliver his opinion upon subjects which he alone understands. And so, one night, I asked him a few questions about the great

European War into which England had just hurled herself.

"What is the cause of the war?" I asked him.

He surveyed me coolly, as if to measure my social status.

"I really haven't the slightest idea," he said at last, indifferently.

I hazarded the opinion that it was the struggle between the Slavs and the Teutons for supremacy in Europe. He shook his head, with a smile.

"The war," he explained, gently, "is between Austria and Serbia."

"But Russia was quite evidently behind Serbia, and Germany at the back of Austria – "

"Entirely due to the fact that some European nations are honorable enough to keep their promises."

I puzzled over this for a moment. Perhaps his words possessed a subtlety which I quite missed.

"And England's action with regard to Belgium?"

"She was forced to enter the struggle because Germany was threatening France by the invasion of Belgium."

"And incidentally, herself?"

"Not at all," replied he, and said no more.

I looked at him in surprise.

"But I mean, the underlying causes of the war!"

"Beyond what I have given, there are none," he continued placidly.

"But upon what was the treaty based which guaranteed Belgium's neutrality?"

"Treaty?" he exclaimed. "Nonsense. There is no treaty in existence guaranteeing Belgian neutrality. England does not make treaties. Surely, even an American is not gullible enough to believe there are anything but secret understandings between the great European Powers?"

"All right," I cried impatiently. "But what do they mean? What is at the bottom of it all?"

"Foreign policy," was the remarkable answer. "Not in

my line. Haven't the least idea. Theoretical stuff, and all that." Contemptuous, he gazed meditatively out of the window.

"But don't you think there is a possibility of popular uprisings as the result of this war?"

"I think not."

"With the anti-war, revolutionary Labor elements so strong, I should think that the prolongation of the war might exhaust their patriotism."

"A Labor party in Europe?" It was a question so full of surprise, so supercilious, that I answered rather hotly.

"In England even. You are by no means free from the fear of revolution there – with England being drawn, as she is, into an offensive war."

"Nonsense," he returned, with a sharp note, such as one uses in reproving a small boy. "You evidently know nothing of my country. Confine your speculations to your own."

"Do you remember the coal strike and the railway strike?" I asked. "Surely not even a Public School and Oxford man is so obtuse as to refuse to recognize the signs of the times!"

"Cambridge," he returned, untouched. "I happen to have been on duty in both strikes."

"Policeman?" I asked.

"No," he answered, with a reproachful look. "No. Lieutenant in the Terr'torials, of course."

"And didn't you see how those strikers felt?"

"I did not. I saw nothing, except that they outnumbered us a hundred to one, and were afraid to fight. And, moreover, you know, revolutions occur only when a people is oppressed."

"Yes – ?" I said.

"And British workingmen are not oppressed. They are paid excellently for persons of their class – "

He continued regularly, placidly, to draw the pipe of his race and station.

"Are you," I said, struck with an idea, "are you by any chance now on your way to England to join the army?"

"Yes," he answered. He never would have told me of his own accord, but I could see it didn't displease him to be discovered.

"What is your idea, in fighting?" I asked.

"I beg pardon!" He was frankly amazed.

"Why do you want to fight the Germans? Is it because of your sympathy with the French?"

"What an extraordinary thing to ask an Englishman! Sympathy with the French! Good God, no!"

"Then why? Hatred of the Germans?"

"Emphatically not. I'm very fond of the Germans. I fight because, well, my people have always been army people."

After that he shut up; nor could I draw from him more than cultivated monosyllables the rest of the journey. He evidently considered that he had exceeded the bounds of taste in so far revealing himself.

As for his opinion of me, the Army Wife told me the next day that he had asked her whether I was a Gentleman.

And so our ways parted at Chicago, he to seek passage back to England. He was a splendid sight as he stepped along the platform, the pink of young English manhood, the quintessence of that famous ruling class that has made itself the greatest empire the world has ever seen – without the least idea what it was doing. He went to glory or the grave, fearless, handsome, unemotional, one hundred and sixty pounds of bone and muscle and gentle blood, with the inside of his head like an Early Victorian drawing-room, all knick-knacks, hair-cloth furniture and drawn blinds. And I had a momentary, guilty idea that perhaps the spirit that conquered India was the same which would wade through fire and blood to get a cold bath in the morning – because it was the Thing to Do.

1916

THE HEAD OF THE FAMILY

On the platform of the observation car I sat down beside a little, chicken-breasted man with protruding green eyes and a retreating chin. He wore Pacific Coast ready-made clothes, shoes with humps on the toes, and from under the narrow brim of a 1913 derby, thin damp locks of hair straggled. Altogether he was a picture of shabby failure, and his weak but friendly grin intensified the effect.

"Pardon me," he said with exaggerated distinctness, and whiskey fumes proceeded from him. "Pardon me. But could you, by any possible chance, tell me when the Cunard boat sails from New York?"

"I couldn't."

"Extraord'n'ry," he mumbled. "Most peculiar. Formerly they published the sailing dates of the Cunard and the White Star in the San Francisco *Examiner*. But for the last three weeks there's been never a word. Possibly" – he peered round at me with an anxious face – "possibly Hearst has refused to allow them in his papers – being pro-German and all that – what? Or they may have withdrawn their ad*vert*isements – adver*tise*ments I should say over here." He grinned half maliciously, half apologetically. *"Cyvis Romainus summ."*

"Cambridge?" I asked. "You must be, for that's the only place where they teach that kind of Latin."

He was pleased. "Yes," he said, "Christ's."

"Going home?" He nodded. "To fight?"

"Yes. That is to say, Royal Army Medical. I'm a doctor." He fumbled rather blindly with some torn letters, and muttered, "I couldn't go it any longer, you see. My two brothers are at the front – Hubert's even been wounded. And I'm the eldest. . . . It's been difficult to decide. I've a letter here somewhere." He shuffled them unavailingly. "Damn! No matter. But I wrote my old tutor – Sargent's his name – and asked his advice. And he answered, 'Drop everything and come at once. England needs every man.' So here I am."

"Of course," said I, "if you feel like it. Married?"

"Yes."

"Children?"

"Children?" he echoed, and smiled waveringly. "No, thank God. I'm not such a rotter as that. There'll be no more to follow like me." Gloomily he looked down at his hands and they shook.

There was nothing to say to that. We were silent for a space, while out from under us spun the gleaming rails, and the cold desert flowed interminably by, dead of fire under the ashen sky.

"Have you been long in America?" I asked finally.

He forgot himself. "Two years and a half. I think I've visited all your States, looking for a place to settle. We went to California finally. I'm now physician in a lumber company." He broke off. "My God! Why do I talk to you like this? I wouldn't say a word if I hadn't two jolts of whiskey in me!" He stopped, and then said in a gentle voice, "I've a Cambridge and London degree – and I'm doctor in a lumber company!"

Now I was brought up in the West, and I appreciated the full force of that. The doctor of a lumber company is equivalent to the doctor on a Fall River steamer, or the house-physician of a Raines-law hotel. He is not paid by the lumber company: he is given a dollar a month for each laborer, deducted from the laborer's pay – and for that "doc" supplies their medical needs. Saw-mills are dangerous places to work, and lumber companies take few precautions against accidents. As for the doctor – well, I knew one who quit after three months of it, some four hundred dollars in debt. No decent, conscientious medical man can afford to be doctor for a lumber company.

"When it's all over," he went on, and a new train of thought flushed his cheeks warm, "there'll be another brass plate up over the family pew in Ansingham Church. I see them all now:

> *Roger Lewellyn, killed in action on board*
> *H.M.S. Victory, Trafalgar, 1805.*
> *Captain Thomas Lewellyn, died of wounds,*
> *Sebastopol, 1856.*
> *Trevor Lewellyn, killed in action,*
> *Ladysmith, 1900.*

"And then," he clapped me on the shoulders, eyes blazing, and shouted ringingly, "and then a shining new plate:

> *Mortimer Lewellyn, R.A.M.C.,*
> *killed on active service, Flanders, 1916.*

"I can see my father stamping into church of a Sunday morning, just a few minutes late, as he always did – the head of the Lewellyn family – the Lewellyn family church – and the curate respectfully halting the Lesson until my father is seated; and my father looking slowly up the line of brass plates that hold the memory of our fighting dead until his eyes strike upon 'Mortimer Lewellyn.' The whole line's clean! The whole line's clean! Isn't that worth dying for? What?" He wiped the sweat from his forehead.

"And your wife," I said. "It must be hard on her to see you go."

He shrugged his shoulders. "Why should she care?" he asked with bitterness, gesticulating. "She has money enough for three months' rent, and then they'll begin paying her the pension. Oh, it settles many things! No more rotten worrying. No more embarrassment. No more keeping up appearances. Three years of shabby living we've had, three years – God!" He mused. "She said it had all been a failure. And perhaps it has been. Perhaps. It's so difficult ever to know afterward whether you've been right or wrong. If I had it to do again, I wonder – "

"It's wasting time to be sorry for what you've done," I ventured, uncomprehending.

He didn't seem to hear me. "She was the daughter of a Devon cattle-breeder, you see. My family couldn't permit *that*. I'm the eldest son, and one day I shall be the head. So," and here his miserable twisted little soul stared straight out of his eyes, "we came to live in America. And so – I'm going home. Don't you see?"

"No, I don't!" I exclaimed heatedly, though I did. "You broke that infernal spell once. Why don't you stick it out? Make yourself a new place, a new family tradition if you will, in this New World, and let that rotten old scaffolding crumble under the feet of its stupid strong men!"

He shook his head and smiled whimsically. "You are an American. You can't understand. You can't. When I first came here I thought I was free. The War shook me up. The War brought it home to me. And then at last I knew that the Family was the important thing. It's in the blood. We cannot get away from it. Why, do you know, we're clean, untouched, unbranded with dishonor all the way back to thirteen hundred! In fifteen ninety-one, under Queen Bess, Richard Lewellyn was High Sheriff of Anglesea, Lewellyn of Ansingham. My father's Richard Lewellyn too: when I write to him I address the letter,

'Richard Lewellyn, J. P., Carnarvonshire.' That's what we mean in England!"

"Why don't you take your wife to England?"

He resented the question, sobering rapidly as he was; but still he answered.

"We hadn't enough money to book us both. Even one of us, for that matter. I've had to cable my father for a passage to Liverpool. And besides, I couldn't bring her to Ansingham. Shall I send her to her people in Devonshire and slink home myself? I can't do that!" He tossed his head proudly, and then suddenly bobbed me a cold little bow. "Forgive my unpardonable bad taste!" said he, and vanished.

I saw him again several times, wandering restlessly up and down the train, or crunched over in his seat reading an article in a medical magazine, which I could see was entitled "The Pathology of War Surgery." Even in the superheated Pullman he wore his threadbare overcoat and battered derby. He was unshaven for days. To me he nodded with distant politeness.

As I passed his seat on the way to lunch I asked him if he were coming into the diner.

"Thanks," he answered stiffly. "I shall go later."

Again at dinner-time I spoke to him.

"Awfully sorry. I've just been."

But I never met him in the diner, and I know now that he never went there. When and how he ate is a mystery.

That evening we stopped for ten minutes at Helena, and I took a few swift turns up and down the platform in the biting winter air. Lewellyn was also walking: we passed each other several times, and then he disappeared. When the train pulled out I went into the washroom, and the first thing I saw was Lewellyn. He sprawled flat on the seat, hat on the floor, coat half off, mouth open wide – snoring. A pint flask, clasped in his slowly relaxing arms, tilted to the rattling of the train, and evil smelling whiskey trickled slimily down the front of him. I set the bottle in the rack and shook him.

"Wha – " he began, and gulped, struggling to a sitting position. "Hel*lo*, hellohellohello!" He looked me carefully up and down and smiled with great cordiality. "I jolly well knew it was you. Sit down. I've a good deal of whiskey in me."

"How's the future head of the Lewellyn family?" I asked jocularly.

"Oh, I've been a rotter, all right," he said, with a sort of reckless gaiety. "But not such a rotter as that. Hubert will be the head of the family. Hubert knows how to play the game – and he's engaged to the Honorable Mary. . . . And now when they think of me they won't have to shut their mouths. No, my boy!" He slapped me on the back. "They'll say 'Mortimer was the eldest, but he was killed in Flanders.' What?"

For a moment he stared straight ahead, imagining things. His weak, eager little face with the bulging eyes, all smudged and covered with soft, meager black whiskers, was transfigured.

"I shall sit down to dinner at Ansingham. Brooks – old Brooks whose father was my grandfather's butler – he'll be sniveling because I'm home again. There'll be only mother and father. I can see the old man as if he were here. He won't ask me why I've come back; he'll simply sit and look at me with those bushy frowning eyes. And mother will be all in black, at foot of the table, with a face as blank as – as that leather-backed chair over there. I can hear her saying, in that quiet, dead voice of hers, 'Hubert is with his regiment at Salonika. Dick is training at Whitchurch. What are *you* going to do, Mortimer?'" Here Lewellyn stood up, and his face took a stern look. "I'm off in the morning, mother!"

And without another word to me he staggered to the door and out. Later I saw a grinning porter and the Pullman conductor hoisting an inert form into the upper berth I knew was his.

Regularly every night after that he got drunk and talked. I got vivid glimpses of the life he knew and loved; of the banquet at Ansingham when his Majesty's Judges came to the County for Assizes week; of his mother visiting her sick villagers like a medieval chatelaine; of flowing ale in the kitchen Christmas Eve, and drunken tenants; of an undergraduate club at Cambridge. Once he rambled about his experience as interne in a London hospital, of weak debauches with medical students, of incessant whiskey and a hand that trembled and trouble in the hospital and at home. Then came his love affair, the regenerating, the healing thing in his life – he seems to have clung to it as a desperate remedy from all this drifting. Adamant opposition from the family – elopement – America. I had to piece together these fragments, for he never talked connectedly. But it gave an impressionistic picture of a life, altogether.

At Chicago we took separate trains, and I lost him.

Five days later there was a knock at the door of my room in New York, and there stood Lewellyn. He was shaved, but his hat and overcoat were even shabbier than before, and his collar was in the last stages of whiteness. He smelled of whiskey.

"Pardon me," he began, entering with an apologetic air. "You remember you gave me your address on the train, and said if you could be of service – "

"But I thought you were sailing. There have been two boats."

"Yes, I know it," he answered vaguely. "But – well – it's a bit humiliating – but I've sent two cables and there's no answer. Has there been time yet, do you think?"

I told him with all the assurance that I could muster that probably war-time conditions were delaying the cable, and asked what I could do for him.

"It's a thing I hate to ask," he hesitated. "And I want you to believe that I shouldn't dream of doing such a thing, except that you're a University man, you know, and so am I, and we are a distinct class, so to speak – brothers, what? I want to cable my father again – but – but – I am temporarily embarrassed. Could you – ?"

I said I would send the cable for him.

He beamed.

"Thanks, awfully. I'll surely pay you when my money comes. Even if it doesn't – I've telegraphed my wife to send twenty dollars of the rent money – "

"If it doesn't?" I echoed. "But surely your father – "

"He might not." Lewellyn smiled and shook his head doubtfully. "He's a quaint old beggar, my father. Showed me the door once, you know. We're a stubborn family."

"But what will you do if he doesn't send it?" I asked. "Back to California?"

"No," he answered thoughtfully. "No, I think not. I imagine I'll stay here. I've done with that out there. She'll be better off without me."

"But how can you stay here? You haven't any money. You haven't – " I was going to say that he hadn't the least chance of getting work. England may need every man, but America doesn't.

"One city is as good as another," said Lewellyn enigmatically.

"Well," I shook hands with him, "if you don't get any answer, let me know. Perhaps I can do something – "

A week later I received a five-dollar bill in an otherwise empty envelope. I telephoned to the steamship offices, but no Doctor Mortimer Lewellyn had sailed on any liner bound for England. . . . Finally, after a search, I found the hotel where he had stayed – an ancient hostelry far downtown, much frequented by out-of-town buyers of wholesale clothing.

"Lewellyn?" said the clerk. "Say, are you a friend of his?

He left here six days ago – didn't pay his bill – we've got his trunk, but there isn't anything in it but dirty shirts."

I wonder if I ought to write to brother Hubert, the future head of the Lewellyn family, Ansingham, Carnarvonshire, England.

1916

EN ROUTE

MEXICAN PICTURES

I. SOLDIERS OF FORTUNE

(Jiminez, 1914)

There, at the side of the plaza, I came upon a little group of five Americans huddled upon a bench. They were ragged beyond belief, all except a slender youth in leggings and a Federal officer's uniform, who wore a crownless Mexican hat. Feet protruded from their shoes, none had more than the remnants of socks, all were unshaven. One mere boy wore his arm in a sling made out of a torn blanket.

They made room for me gladly, crowded around, cried how good it was to see another American among all these damned greasers.

"What are you fellows doing here?" I asked.

"We're soldiers of fortune!" said the boy with the wounded arm. "Aw – !" interrupted another. "Soldiers of. . . .!"

"Ye see it's this way," began the soldierly looking youth. "We've been fighting right along in the Brigada Zaragosa – was in the battle of Ojinaga and everything. And now comes an order from Villa to discharge all the Americans in the ranks and ship 'em back to the border. Ain't that a hell of a note?"

"Last night they gave us our honorable discharges and

threw us out of the *cuartel*," said a one-legged man with red hair.

"And we ain't had any place to sleep and nothing to eat – " broke in a little gray-eyed boy whom they called major.

"Don't try and panhandle the guy!" rebuked the soldier, indignantly. "Ain't we each going to get fifty Mex. in the morning?"

We adjourned for a short time to a near-by restaurant, and when we returned I asked them what they were going to do?

"The old U. S. for mine," breathed a good-looking black Irishman who hadn't spoken before. "I'm going back to San Fran. and drive a truck again. I'm sick of greasers, bad food, and bad fighting."

"I got two honorable discharges from the United States army," announced the soldierly youth proudly. "Served through the Spanish war, I did. I'm the only soldier in this bunch." The others sneered and cursed sullenly. "Guess I'll re-enlist when I get over the border."

"Not for mine," said the one-legged man. "I'm wanted for two murder charges – I didn't do it, I swear to God I didn't – it was a frame-up. But a poor guy hasn't got a chance in the United States. When they ain't framing up some fake charge against me, they jail me for a 'vag.' I'm all right, though," he went on earnestly. "I'm a hard-working man, only I can't get no job."

The major raised his hard little face and cruel eyes. "I got out of a reform-school in Wisconsin," he said, "and I guess there's some cops waiting for me in El Paso. I always wanted to kill somebody with a gun, and I done it at Ojinaga, and I ain't got a bellyful yet. They told us we could stay if we signed Mex. citizenship papers; I guess I'll sign tomorrow morning."

"The hell you will," cried the others. "That's a rotten thing to do. Suppose we get intervention and you have to shoot against your own people. You won't catch me signing myself away to be a greaser."

"That's easy fixed," said the major. "When I go back to the States I leave my own name here. I'm going to stay down here till I get enough of a stake to go back to Georgia and start a child-labor factory."

The other boy had suddenly burst into tears. "I got my arm shot through in Ojinaga," he sobbed, "and now they're turning me loose without any money, and I can't work. When I get to El Paso the cops'll jail me and I'll have to write my dad to come and take me home to California. I run away from there last year," he explained.

"Look here," I advised, "you had better not stay down here if Villa wants Americans out of the ranks. Being a Mexican citizen won't help you if intervention comes."

"Perhaps you're right," agreed the major thoughtfully. "Aw, quit your bawling, Jack! I guess I'll beat it over to Galveston and get on a South American boat. They say there's a revolution started in Peru."

The soldier was about thirty, the Irishman twenty-five, and the three others somewhere between sixteen and eighteen.

"What did you fellows come down here for?" I asked.

"Excitement!" answered the soldier and the Irishman, grinning.

The three boys looked at me with eager, earnest faces, drawn with hunger and hardship. "Loot!" they said simultaneously.

I cast an eye at their tattered garments, at the throngs of ragged volunteers parading around the plaza, who hadn't been paid for months, and restrained a violent impulse to shout with mirth. . . . Poor misfits in a passionate country, despising the cause for which they were fighting, sneering at the gaiety of a poverty-stricken people they could never understand! As I went away I asked:

"By the way, what company did you fellows belong to? What did you call yourselves?"

The red-haired youth answered. "The Foreign Legion," he said.

II. PEONS

(Beyond Jiminez)

We entered the desert, winding over a series of rolling plains, sandy and covered with black mesquit, with here and there an occasional cactus. . . . Night gathered straight above in the cloudless zenith, while all the skyline still was luminous with clear light, and then the light of day snuffed out, and stars burst out in the dome of heaven like a rocket.

Toward midnight we discovered that the road upon which we were traveling suddenly petered out in a dense mesquit thicket. Somewhere we had turned off the *Camino Real*. The mules were worn out. There was nothing for it but a "dry camp."

Now we had unharnessed the mules and fed them, and were lighting our fire, when somewhere in the dense thicket of chapparal stealthy footsteps sounded.

"Who lives?" said Antonio.

There was a little shuffling noise out in the bush, and then a voice.

"Whose party are you?" it asked hesitantly.

"*Maderistas*," answered Antonio. "Pass!"

Two vague shapes materialized on the edge of the firelight glow, almost without a sound. Two peons, we saw as soon as they came close, wrapped tightly in their torn blankets. One was an old, wrinkled, bent man wearing homemade sandals, his trousers hanging in rags upon his shrunken legs; the other a very tall, barefooted youth. Friendly, warm as sunlight, eagerly curious as children, they came forward, holding out their hands. We shook hands with each of them in turn, greeting them with elaborate Mexican courtesy.

At first they politely refused our invitation to dine, but after much urging we finally persuaded them to accept a few tortillas and chile. It was ludicrous and pitiful to see how wretchedly hungry they were, and how they attempted to conceal it from us.

After dinner, when they had brought us a bucket of water out of sheer kindly thoughtfulness, they stood for a while by our fire, smoking our cigarettes and holding out their hands to the blaze. I remember how their *serapes* hung from their shoulders, open in front so the grateful warmth could reach their thin bodies – and how gnarled and ancient were the old man's outstretched hands, and how the ruddy light glowed on the other's throat, and kindled fires in his big eyes. . . . I suddenly conceived these two human beings as symbols of Mexico – courteous, loving, patient, poor, so long slaves, so full of dreams, so soon to be free.

"When we first saw your wagon coming here," said the old man, smiling, "our hearts sank within us. We thought you were soldiers, come, perhaps, to take away our last few goats. So many soldiers have come in the last few years – so many. It is mostly the Federals – the *Maderistas* do not come unless they are hungry themselves. Poor *Maderistas!*"

"Ay," said the young man, "my brother that I loved very much died in the eleven days' fighting around Torreon. Thousands have died in Mexico, and still more thousands shall fall. Three years – it is long for war in a land. Too long."

The old man murmured, *"Valgame Dios!"*

"But there shall come a day – " said the young man.

"It is said," remarked the old man quaveringly, "that the United States of the North covets our country – that gringo soldiers will come and take away my goats in the end. . . ."

"The rich Americanos want to rob us," said the young man, "just as the rich Mexicans want to rob us."

The old man shivered and drew his wasted body nearer to the fire. "I have often wondered," he said mildly, "why the rich, having so much, want so much. The poor, who have nothing, want so very little. Only a few goats. . . ."

His *compadre* lifted his chin like a noble, smiling gently. "I have never been out of this little country here – not even to Jiminez," he said. "But they tell me that there are many rich lands to the north and south and east. But this is my land and I love it. For the years of me and my father and grandfather, the rich men have gathered in the corn and held it in their clenched fists before our mouths. And only blood will make them open their hands to their brothers."

The fire died down. . . .

1914

THE WORLD WELL LOST

The Serbian town of Obrenovatz is a cluster of red tile roofs and white bulbous towers, hidden in green trees on a belt of land, around which sweeps the river Sava in a wide curve. Behind, the green hills of Serbia topple to blue ranges of mountains, upon whose summits heaps of dead bodies lie still unburied, among the stumps of trees riddled with machine-gun fire; and half-starved dogs battle there ghoulishly with the vultures. Half a mile away on the bank of the yellow river the peasant soldiers stand knee-deep in inundated trenches, firing at the Austrians three hundred yards away on the other side. Between, the rich hills of Bosnia sweep westward forever like sea-swells, hiding the big guns that cover Obrenovatz with the menace of destruction. The town itself is built on a little rise of ground, surrounded by flooded marshes when the river is high, where the sacred storks stalk seriously among the rushes, contemptuous of battles. All the hills are alive with vivid new leaves and plum-tree blossoms like smoke. The earth rustles with a million tiny thrills, the pushing of pale-green shoots and the bursting of buds; the world steams with spring. And regular as clockwork, the crack of desultory shots rises unnoticed into the lazy air. For nine months it has been so, and the sounds of war have become a part of the great chorus of nature.

We had dinner with the officers of the Staff – good-natured giants who were peasants and sons of peasants. The orderly who fell upon his knees to brush our shoes and stood so stiffly pouring water over our hands, and the private soldiers who waited on us at dinner with such smart civility, came in and sat down when coffee was served, and were introduced all around. They were intimate friends of the colonel.

After dinner somebody produced a bottle of cognac and a box of real Havana cigars – which Iovanovitch laughingly said had been captured from the Austrians two weeks before – and we strolled out to visit the batteries.

Westward over the Bosnian hills a pale spring sun hung low in a shallow sky of turquoise green. Line after line the little clouds burned red-golden, scarlet, vermilion, pale pink and gray, all up the tremendous arch of sky. Drowsy birds twittered, and a soft fresh wind came up out of the west.

Iovanovitch turned to me:

"You wanted to talk to a Serbian Socialist," he said. "Well, you'll have the chance. The captain in command of the battery we are going to see is leader of one of the Serbian Socialist parties – or at least he was, in the days of peace. No, I don't know what his doctrines are; I am a Young Radical myself," he laughed. "We believe in the Great Serbian Empire."

"If all Socialists were like Takits," said the colonel, puffing comfortably at his cigar, "I wouldn't have a thing to say against Socialism."

In a deep trench, curved in half-moon shape across the corner of a field, four six-inch guns crouched behind a screen of young willows. There was a roof over them almost on the level with the field, and on this roof sods had been laid and grass and bushes were growing, to hide them from aeroplanes. At the sentry's staccato challenge the colonel answered, and hailed, "Takits!" Out of the gunpits came a man, muddy to the knees and without a hat. He was tall and broad; his faded uniform hung upon him as if once he had been stout; a thick, unkempt beard covered his face to the cheekbones, and his eyes were quiet and direct.

They said something to him in Serbian and he laughed.

"So," he said, turning to me with a twinkle in his eye, and speaking French that halted and hesitated like a thing long unused. "So. You are interested in Socialism?"

I said I was. "They tell me you were a Socialist leader in this country."

"I *was*," he said, emphasizing the past tense. "And now – "

"Now," interrupted the colonel, "he is a patriot and a good soldier."

"Just say 'a good soldier,'" said Takits, and I thought there was a shade of bitterness in his voice. "Forgive me if I speak bad French. It is long since I have talked to foreigners – though I once made speeches in French – "

"And Socialism?" I asked.

"Well, I will tell you," he began slowly. "Walk with me a little." He put his arm under mine and scowled at the earth. Suddenly he turned swiftly, preoccupied, and shouted to some one invisible in the pit: "Peter! Oil breechblock number one gun!"

The others strolled on ahead, laughing and throwing remarks over their shoulders the way men do who have dined and are content. Night rushed up the west and quenched those shining clouds, drawing her train of stars like a robe to cover all heaven. Somewhere in the distant trenches voices sang a quavering Macedonian song about the glories of the Empire of the Tsar Stefan Dushan, and an accompanying violin scratched and squeaked under the hand of a gipsy *gooslar*. On the dim slope of a hill far across the river in the enemy's country a spark of flame quivered red. . . .

"You see, in our country it is different than in yours," began Takits. "Here we have no rich men and no industrial population, so we are not ready, I think, for the immense combining of the workers to oppose the concentration of capital in the hands of the few." He stopped a moment, and then chuckled, "You have no idea how strange it feels to be talking like this again! . . .

"Our party was formed then to apply the principles of Socialism to the conditions of this country – a country of peasants who all own their land. We are naturally communists, we Serbians. In every village you will see the houses of the rich *zadrugas* – many generations of the same family, with all their connections by marriage, who have pooled their property and hold it in common. We didn't want to waste time with the International. It would hinder us – block our program: which was, to get into the hands of the people who produced everything and owned all the means of production, the means of distribution, too. The political program was simpler; we aimed at a real democracy by means of the widest possible suffrage, the initiative, referendum and recall. You see, in the Balkans a great gulf separates the ambitious politicians in power and the masses of the people who elect them. Politics is getting to be a separate profession, closed to all but scheming lawyers. This class we wanted to destroy. We did not believe in the General Strike, and the great oppressed industrial population of the world could do nothing with us, except use us for the furtherance of their economic programs, which had nothing to do with conditions in Serbia."

"You opposed war?"

He nodded. "We were against war – " he began, then stopped short and burst out laughing. "Do you know I had forgotten all that. . . . We thought the peasants, the people of Serbia, could stop war any time if they wanted to, by simply refusing to fight. God! There were only a few of us – not a great solid working-class as in Germany and France – but we thought it could be done."

"And now – what do you believe?"

Takits turned slowly to me, and his eyes were tragic and bitter. "I don't know. I don't know. It was myself before the war who spoke to you just now. What a shock it was to hear my voice saying those old, outworn things! They are so meaningless now! I have come to think that it has all to be done over again – the upbuilding of civilization. Again we must learn to till the soil, to live together under a common government, to make friends across frontiers with other races, who have become once more only dark, evil faces and speakers of tongues not our own. This world has become a place of chaos, as it was in the Dark Ages; and yet we live, have our work to do, feel happiness on a clear day and sadness when it rains. These are more important than anything just now. Afterward will come the long pull up from barbarism to a time when men think and reason and consciously organize their lives again. . . . But that will not be in our time. I shall die without seeing it – the world we loved and lost."

He turned to me with extraordinary emotion, eyes blazing and dark, and gripped my arm tensely. "Here is the point – the tragic point. Once I was a lawyer. The other day the Colonel asked me about some common legal point, and *I had forgotten it.* When I talked with you about my party, I discovered again that all was vague – nebulous. You noticed how obscure and general it was, didn't you? Well, *I have forgotten my arguments, and I have lost my faith.*

"For four years now I have been fighting in the Serbian army. At first I hated it, wanted to stop, was oppressed by the *unreasonableness* of it all. Now it is my job, my life. I spend all day thinking of those guns; I lie awake at night worrying about the men of the battery – whether So-and-So will stand his watch without carelessness, whether I shall need fresh horses in place of the lame ones in the gun-teams, what can be done to correct the slight recoiling-fault of number three. These things and my food, my bed, the weather – that is life to me. When I go home on leave to visit my wife and children, their existence seems so tame, so removed from the realities. I get bored very soon, and am relieved when the time comes to return to my friends here, my work – my guns. . . . That is the horrible thing."

He ceased, and we walked along in silence. A stork on great pinions came flapping down upon the roof of the cottage where he had his nest. From far down the river a sudden ripple of rifle-shots broke out inexplicably, and ended with sharp silence.

1916

REVOLUTIONARY
VIGNETTES

I. ON THE EVE

1. En Route to the Front

The commandant of the Baltic station set aside a separate first-class compartment for the "American Mission," as he called us. An Orthodox priest, bound on volunteer priestly duty to the trenches, humbly begged the honor of traveling in our company. He was a big, healthy man, with a wide, simple Russian face, a gentle smile, an enormous reddish beard, and an insatiable desire for conversation.

"*Eto vierno!* It's true!" he said, with the suspicion of a sigh. "The revolution has weakened the hold of the church on the masses of the people. On the caps of the reserves used to be a cross and the words, '*Za verou, tsaria, i otechestvo*' – 'For faith, tsar, and fatherland.' Well, they scratched out the 'faith' along with the rest. . . ." He shook his head. "In the old text of the church prayers God was referred to as 'Tsar of Heaven,' and the Virgin as 'Tsarina.' We've had to leave that out – the people won't have God insulted, they say. . . ."

We went on to speak of his work in the armies, and his face grew infinitely tender.

"During regimental prayer the priest prays for peace to all nations. Whereupon the soldiers cry out, 'Add "without annexations or indemnities!"' Then we pray for

115

all those who are traveling, for the sick and the suffering; and the soldiers cry, 'Pray also for the deserters!' . . . Woe to the priest who refuses to pray the soldiers' prayer!"

At every station the train made a long halt to allow the passengers time for many glasses of tea and a great gulping of food, in the cheerful, steamy clatter of crowded waiting rooms. In between times utter strangers, officers and civilians drifted in.

The priest lived in Tashkent, in the Trans-Caspia, where he had a wife and five children. He told about the singular institution of the Thieves' Bureau, where persons who had been robbed could go and recover their property by paying its value, less 20 per cent discount for cash. A thin little school-teacher described the Thieves' Convention held in Rostov-on-Don this summer with delegates from all over Russia, which despatched a formal protest to the Government against the rapacity and venality of the police. And a fat *polkovnik* spoke of the Convention of German and Austrian Prisoners of War, in Moscow, which demanded the eight-hour workday – and got it!

Rumor had it that the armies at the front would leave the trenches and go home for the feast of *Pakrov,* the first of October – then only four days off. Each one was concerned about this immense threat of dissolution. . . . What if the millions of Russian soldiers were simply to stop fighting and start for the cities, for the capital, for their villages? The old *polkovnik* muttered, "We are lost. Russia is defeated. And besides, life is so uncomfortable now that it is not worth living. Why not finish everything?" With whom the French-speaking officer, revolutionist by theory, debated hotly but courteously. The priest told a very simple Rabelaisian story about a soldier who seduced a peasant girl by promising that her child would be a general. . . .

It grew late, the lights were dim and intermittent, and there was no heat in the car. The priest shivered. "Well," he said, finally, his teeth chattering, "it is too cold to stay awake!" And with that he lay down just as he was, without any covering but his long skirts, and immediately fell to snoring. . . .

Very early in the morning we awoke, stiff and numb. The sun sparkled through the frosty windows. A small boy came through with tea – chocolate candy in place of sugar. The train was poking down across rich Estland. . . .

2. The Iskosol* at Venden

In a large bare room on the second floor, amid the clack of busy stenographers and the come-and-go of couriers and deputations, functioned the nerve-center of the Twelfth Army, the spontaneous democratic organization created by the soldiers at the outbreak of the Revolution. A handsome young lieutenant, with Jewish features, stood behind a table, running his hand through his gray-streaked hair worriedly, while a torrent of agitated complaint beat upon him. Four delegations from the regiments in the trenches, mostly soldiers, with a couple of officers mixed in, were appealing to the Iskosol all at once; one regiment was almost without boots – the Iskosol had promised six hundred pairs and had only delivered sixty; a very ragged private spokesman for another committee complained that the artillery had been given their winter fur coats, but the cavalry was still in summer uniform. . . . One sub-officer, a mere boy, kept shouting angrily that the Iskosol buzzed around a good deal, but nothing seemed to get done.

"*Da, da!*" responded the officer vaguely, "Yes, yes. *S'chass, s'chass.* I will write immediately to the Commissariat. . . ."

* The soldiers' revolutionary self-governing organization, then in its first stages.

On a little table were piled heaps of pamphlets and newspapers, among which I noticed Elisée Réclus' *Anarchy and the Church.* A soldier sat in a broken chair nearby, reading aloud the *Isvestia* – official organ of the Petrograd Executive Committee of the All-Russian Soviets – about the formation of the new government; and as he declaimed the names of the Cadet ministers, the listeners gave vent to laughter and ironical "hoorahs." Near the window stood Voitinsky, assistant Commissar of the Twelfth Army, with his semi-military coat buttoned up to his chin – a little man whose blue eyes snapped behind thick glasses, with bristling red hair and beard; he who was a famous exile in Siberia, and the author of *Smertniki,* a book more terrible than *The Seven Who Were Hanged.*

"My job," he told us, "is to build a military machine which will retake Riga. But conditions here are desperate. The army lacks everything – food, clothes, boots, munitions. The roads are awful, and it has been raining steadily for two weeks. The horses of the transport are underfed and worn out, and it is all they can do to haul enough bread to keep us from starving. But the most serious lack at the front, more serious than the lack of food and clothes, is the lack of boots, pamphlets and newspapers.

"You see – since the revolution the army has absorbed tons of literature, propaganda, and has a gnawing hunger; and now all that is cut off. We not only permit, but encourage the importation of all kinds of literature in the army – it is necessary in order to keep up the spirits of the troops. Since the Kornilov affair, and especially since the Democratic Congress, the soldiers have been very uneasy. Yes, many have simply laid down their arms and gone home. The Russian army is sick of war...."

Voitinsky had had no sleep for thirty-six hours. Yet he fairly radiated quick energy as he saluted and ran down the steps to his mud-covered automobile – bound on a

forty-mile ride through the deep mud, in the shadow of
the coming rainstorm, to judge a dispute between officers
and soldiers. . . .

3. At Venden

Outside it was raining, and the mud of the streets had
been tracked on the sidewalks by thousands of boots until
it was difficult to walk. The city was darkened against
hostile aeroplanes; only chinks of light gleamed from
shutters, and blinds glowed dull red. The narrow street
made unexpected turns. In the dark we hurtled incessant
passing soldiers, spangled with cigarette-lights. Close by
passed a series of great trucks, some army-transport, rushing down in the black gloom with a noise like thunder,
and a fan-like spray of ooze. Right before me someone
scratched a match, and I saw a soldier pasting a white
paper on a wall. Our guide, one of the Iskosol, gave an
exclamation and ran up, flashing an electric torch. We
read:

Comrade Soldiers!
The Venden Soviet of Workmen's and Soldiers'
Deputies has arranged for Thursday, September 28,
at 4 o'clock in the park, a MEETING. . . .

At the little hotel the proprietor, half hostile, half
greedy-frightened, said that there were no rooms.
"How about that room?" asked our friend, pointing.
"That is the commandant's room," he replied, gruffly.
"The Iskosol takes it," said the other. We got it.
It was an old Lettish peasant woman who brought us
tea, and peered at us out of her bleary eyes, rubbing her
hand and babbling German. "You are foreigners," she
said, "glory to God. These Russians are dirty folk, and

they do not pay." She leaned down and hoarsely whispered: "Oh, if the Germans would only hurry. We respectable folk all want the Germans to come here!"

And through the shut wooden blinds, as we settled down to sleep, we could hear the far-off thud-booming of the German cannon hammering on the thin, ill-clad, underfed Russian lines, torn by doubts, fears, distrust, dying and rotting out there in the rain because they were told that the Revolution would be saved thereby. . . .

4. En Route from the Front

As we sat on the platform waiting for the Petrograd train, it occurred to [Albert Rhys] Williams that we might as well give away our superfluous cigarettes. Accordingly he sat down on a trunk and held out a big box, making generous sounds. There must have been several hundred soldiers around. A few came hesitantly and helped themselves, but the rest held aloof, and soon Williams sat alone in the midst of an everwidening circle. The soldiers were gathered in groups, talking in low tones.

Suddenly he saw coming towards him a committee of three privates, carrying rifles with fixed bayonets, and looking dangerous. "Who are you?" the leader asked. "Why are you giving away cigarettes? Are you a German spy, trying to bribe the Russian revolutionary army?"

All over the platform the crowd followed, slowly packing itself around Williams and the committee, muttering angrily – ready to tear him to pieces.

We were packed into the train too tight to move. In compartments meant for six people, twelve were jammed, and there was such a crowd in the aisles that no one could pass. On the roof of the car a hundred soldiers stamped their feet and sang shrill songs in the freezing night air.

Inside all the windows were shut, everybody smoked, there was universal conversation.

At Valk some gay young Red Cross nurses and young officers climbed in at the windows, with candy, bottles of vodka, cheese, sausages, and all the materials for a feast. By some miracle, they wedged themselves among us and began to make merry. They grew amorous, kissing and fondling each other. In our compartment two couples fell to embracing, half lying upon the seats. Somebody pulled the black shade over the lights; another shut the door. It was a debauch, with the rest of us looking on. . . .

In the upper berth lay a young captain, coughing incessantly and terribly. Every little while he lifted his wasted face and spat blood into a handkerchief. And over and over he cried: "The Russians are animals!"

Above the roaring of the train, coughing, bacchic cries, quarrels, all through the night one could hear the feet of ragged soldiers pounding on the roof, rhythmically, and their nasal singing. . . .

September, 1917

Fragments from an account of a visit to the Riga front just prior to the October Revolution.

II. THE I.W.W. TRIAL AT CHICAGO

Small on the huge bench sits a wasted man with untidy white hair, an emaciated face in which two burning eyes are set like jewels, parchment skin split by a crack for a mouth; the face of Andrew Jackson three years dead. This is Judge Kenesaw Mountain Landis. . . .

Upon this man has devolved the historic role of trying the Social Revolution.

In many ways a most unusual trial. When the judge enters the court-room after recess no one rises – he himself has abolished the pompous formality. He sits without robes, in an ordinary business suit, and often leaves the bench to come down and perch on the step of the jury box. By his personal order, spittoons are placed beside the prisoners' seats, so they can while away the long day with a chaw, and they are permitted, also, to take off their coats, move around, read newspapers.

As for the prisoners, I doubt if ever in history there has been a sight just like them. One hundred and one lumber-jacks, harvest-hands, miners, editors; one hundred and one who believe that the wealth of the world belongs to him who creates it.

Most of our American social revolutionists are in

the sedentary trades – garment-workers, textile-workers, printers. At least, so it seems to us, in the great cities. Your miners, your steel and iron workers, building-trades, railroad workers – all these belong to the A. F. of L., which believes in the capitalist system as strongly as J. P. Morgan does. But these Hundred and One are out-door men, hardrock blasters, tree-fellers, wheat-binders, longshoremen, the boys who do the strong work of the world. They are scarred all over with the wounds of industry – and the wounds of society's hatred. They aren't afraid of anything. They are the kind of men the capitalist points to as he drives past some great building they are putting up, or some huge bridge they are throwing over a river:

"There," he says, "that's the kind of workingmen we want in this country. Men that know their job and work at it, instead of going around talking bosh about the class struggle."

They know their job, and work at it. But strangely enough they believe in the Social Revolution too. . . .

They file in, the ninety-odd who are still in jail, greeting their friends as they pass; and there they are joined by the others, those who are out on bail. . . .

There goes Big Bill Haywood, with his black Stetson above a face like a scarred mountain; Ralph Chaplin, looking like Jack London in his youth; Reddy Doran, of kindly pugnacious countenance, and a mop of bright red hair falling over the green eye-shade he always wears; Harrison George, whose forehead is lined with hard thinking; Sam Scarlett, who might have been a yeoman at Crécy; George Andreytchine, his eyes full of Slav storm; Charley Ashleigh, fastidious, sophisticated, with the expression of a well-bred Puck; Grover Perry, young, stony-faced after the manner of the West; Jim Thompson, John Foss, J. A. MacDonald; Boose, Prancner, Rothfisher, Johanson, Lossiev. . . .

Inside the rail of the court-room, crowded together,

many in their shirt-sleeves, some reading papers, one or two stretched out asleep, some sitting, some standing up; the faces of workers and fighters, for the most part, also the faces of orators, of poets, the sensitive and passionate faces of foreigners – but all strong faces, all faces of men inspired, somehow; many scarred, few bitter. There could not be gathered together in America one hundred and one men more fit to stand for the Social Revolution. People going into that court-room say, "It's more like a convention than a trial!"

To me, fresh from Russia, the scene was strangely familiar. For a long time I was puzzled at the feeling of having witnessed it all before; then suddenly it flashed upon me.

The I. W. W. trial in the Federal court-room of Chicago looked like a meeting of the Central Executive Committee of the All-Russian Soviets of Workers' Deputies in Petrograd! I could not get it into my head that these men were on trial. They were not at all cringing, or frightened, but confident, interested, humanly understanding ... like the Bolshevik Revolutionary Tribunal.... For a moment it seemed to me that I was watching the Central Committee of the American Soviets trying Judge Landis for – well, say counter-revolution.

1918

ALMOST THIRTY

I am twenty-nine years old, and I know that this is the end of a part of my life, the end of youth. Sometimes it seems to me the end of the world's youth too; certainly the Great War has done something to us all. But it is also the beginning of a new phase of life, and the world we live in is so full of swift change and color and meaning that I can hardly keep from imagining the splendid and terrible possibilities of the time to come. The last 10 years I've gone up and down the earth drinking in experience, fighting and loving, seeing and hearing and testing things. I've traveled all over Europe, and to the borders of the East, and down in Mexico, having adventures; seeing men killed and broken, victorious and laughing, men with visions and men with a sense of humor. I've watched civilization change and broaden and sweeten in my lifetime; and I've watched it wither and crumble in the red blast of war. And war I have seen, too, in the trenches, with the armies. I'm not quite sick of seeing yet, but soon I will be—I know that. My future life will not be what it has been. And so I want to stop a minute, and look back, and get my bearings.

A great deal of my boyhood was illness and physical

125

weakness, and I was never really well until my sixteenth year. The beginning of my remembered life was a turmoil of imaginings—formless perceptions of beauty, which broke forth in voluminous verses, sensations of fear, of tenderness of pain. Then came a period of intense emotion, in which I endowed certain girls with the attributes of Guinevere, and had a vision of Galahad and the Sangraal in the sky over the football field; a furious energy drove me to all kinds of bodily and mental exercise, without any particular direction—except that I felt sure I was going to be a great poet and novelist. After that I was increasingly active and restless, more ambitious of place and power, less exalted, scattering myself in a hundred different directions; life became a beloved moving picture, thought about only in brilliant flashes, conceived as emotion and sensation. And now, almost 30, some of that old superabundant vitality is gone, and with it the all-sufficient joy of mere living. A good many of my beliefs have got twisted by the Great War. I am weakened by a serious operation. Some things I think I have settled, but in other ways I am back where I started—a turmoil of imaginings.

I must find myself again. Some men seem to get their direction early, to grow naturally and with little change to the thing they are to be. I have no idea what I shall be or do one month from now. Whenever I have tried to become some one thing, I have failed; it is only by drifting with the wind that I have found myself, and plunged joyously into a new role. I have discovered that I am only happy when I'm working hard at something I like. I never stuck long at anything I didn't like, and now I couldn't if I wanted to; on the other hand, there are very few things I don't get some fun out of, if only the novelty of experience. I love people, except the well-fed smug, and am interested in all new things and all the beautiful old things they do. I love beauty and chance and change, but less now in the external world and more in my mind. I suppose I'll always be a Romanticist.

From the very beginning my excitable imagination fed on fantasy. I still remember my grandfather's house, where I was born—a lordly gray mansion modeled on a French chateau, with its immense park, its formal gardens, lawns, stables, greenhouses and glass grape-arbor, the tame deer among the trees. All that remains to me of my grandfather is his majestic height, his long slim fingers and the polished courtesy of his manners. He had come around the Horn in a sailing ship when the West Coast was the wild frontier, made his pile and lived with Russian lavishness. Portland was less than 30 years old, a little town carved out of the Oregon forests, with streets deep in mud and the wilderness coming down close around it. Through this my grandfather drove his blooded horses to his smart carriages, imported from the East—and from Europe—with liveried coachmen and footmen on the box. The lawn terrace below the house was surrounded on three sides by great fir trees, up whose sides ran gas-pipes grown over with bark; on summer evenings canvas was laid on the turf, and people danced, illuminated by flaming jets which seemed to spout from the trees. There was something fantastic in all that.

Then we were poor, living in a little house down in the town, with a crowd of gay young people around my gay young father and mother. My head was full of fairy stories and tales of giants, witches and dragons, and I invented a monster called Hormuz, who lived in the woods behind the town and devoured little children—with which I terrified the small boys and girls of the neighborhood and incidentally myself. Almost all the servants in those days were Chinese, who stayed for years, at last getting to be almost members of the family. They brought ghosts and superstitions into the house, and the tang of bloody feuds among themselves, idols and foods and drinks, strange customs and ceremonies; half-affectionate, half-contemptuous, wholly independent, and withal outlandish, they have left me a memory of pig-tails and gongs and fluttering red paper. And there was my uncle, a romantic figure who played at coffee-planting in Central America, mixed in revolutions, and sometimes blew in, tanned and bearded and speaking "spigotty" like a *mestizo*. Once the tale ran that he had helped to lead a revolution that captured Guatemala for a few brief days, and was made Secretary of State; the first thing he did was to appropriate the funds of the National Treasury to give a grand state ball, and then he declared war on the German Empire—because he had flunked his German course in college. Later he went out to the Philippines as a volunteer in the Spanish War—and the tale of how he was made King of Guam is still told with shouts of mirth by the veterans of the Second Oregon.

My mother, who has always encouraged me in the things I wanted to do, taught me to read. I don't know when that was, but I remember the orgy of books I plunged into. History was my passion, kings strutting about and the armored ranks of men-at-arms clashing forward in close ranks against a hail of cloth-yard shafts; but I was equally enamored of Mark Twain, and Bill Nye, and Blackmore's *Lorna Doone*, and Webster's Unabridged Dictionary, and *The Arabian Nights*, and the *Tales of the Round Table*. What I didn't understand, my imagination interpreted. At the age of nine I began to write a Comic History of the United States—after Bill Nye—and I think it was then I made up my mind to be a writer.

About that time we moved to an apartment hotel, and I went to school. Those first few years of school stimulated my ambition to learn; but since then the curricula of schools and colleges have meant little to me. I've always been an indifferent student, to say the least, except when some subject like elementary chemistry, or English poetry, or composition caught my imagination—or the personality of some great teacher, like Professor Copeland of Harvard. Why should I have been interested in the stupid education of our time? We take young soaring imaginations, consumed with curiosity about the life they see all around, and feed them with dead technique; the flawless purity of Washington, Lincoln's humdrum chivalry, our dull and virtuous history and England's honest glory; Addison's graceful style as an essayist, Goldsmith celebrating the rural clergy of the eighteenth century, Dr. Johnson at his most vapid, and George Eliot's *Silas Marner*; Macaulay, and the sonorous oratings of Edmund Burke; and in Latin, Caesar's Gallic guide-book, and Cicero's mouthings about Roman politics. And the teachers! Men and women— usually women—whose chief qualification is that they can plough steadily through a dull round of dates, acts, half-truths and rules for style, without questioning, without interpreting and without seeing how ridiculously unlike the world their teachings are. I have forgotten most of it, forced on me before I was ready; what I do know came mostly from books I had the curiosity to read outside school hours. And many fine things I have had to force myself to explore again, because school once spoiled them for me.

But in going to school I first entered the world of my fellows, and the social experience meant more and more to me until it almost crowded out the study side altogether. I can still see the school playground full of running and shouting and clamoring boys, and feel as I felt then when they stopped here and there to look at me, a new boy, with curious and insolent eyes, I was small though, and not very well, and at the beginning I didn't mix much with them. . . . But after school was out there were great doings, which were too exciting to keep out of. The town was divided into districts, ruled over by gangs of boys in a constant state of fierce warfare. I belonged to the Fourteenth Street gang, whose chief was a tall, curly-headed

Irish boy who lived across the street—he is now a policeman. My best friend could make sounds like a bugle, and he was trumpeter. Standing in the middle of the street he would blow, and in a minute boys would come swarming to him, tearing up lawns and making mudballs as they came. Then we'd go running and shouting up the hill to give battle to the Montgomery Street gang, or beat off their attack. ... And there were the wooded hills behind the town, where Indians and bears and outlaws might be lurking to be trailed by our scouts and Robin Hoods.

Both my mother's parents and my father came from upper New York State, and when I was 10 years old my mother and my brother and I went East to visit them. We spent a summer month at Plymouth, Massachusetts, visited New York (I still remember the awful summer heat, the vermin in our boarding houses and the steam-engines on the Elevated), and were in Washington when the *Maine* blew up and the first volunteers left for the Spanish War.

Then I was back in Portland, in a new house, settling into the life of school and play. We had a theatre in our attic, where we acted over our plays, and we built scenic railways in the yard, and log cabins in the woods back of town. I had a number of highly colored schemes for getting adventure and wealth at the same time. For instance, I once began to dig a tunnel from our house to school, about a mile away; we were going to steal two sheep and hide them in the tunnel, and these two sheep were going to have children, and so on, until a large flock had gathered—then we'd sell them. My brother and I had a pony, and we went on camping trips back in the woods, and sailing and swimming and camping up the Willamette River. I began to write poetry, too, and read voraciously everything I could get hold of, from Edwin Arnold's *Light of Asia* and Marie Corelli, to Scott and Stevenson and Sir Thomas Malory.

But with all this I wasn't entirely happy. I was often ill.

Outside of a few friends, I wasn't a success with the boys. I hadn't strength or fight enough to be good at athletics— except swimming, which I have always loved; and I was a good deal of a physical coward. I would sneak out over the back fence to avoid boys who were "laying" for me, or who I thought were "laying" for me. Sometimes I fought, when I couldn't help myself, and sometimes even won; but I preferred to be called a coward than fight. I hated pain. My imagination conjured up horrible things that would happen to me, and I simply ran away. One time, when I was on the editorial board of the school paper, a boy I was afraid of warned me not to publish a joking paragraph I had written about him—and I didn't. . . . My way to school lay through a sort of slum district, called Goose Hollow, peopled with brutal Irish boys, many of whom grew up to be prizefighters and baseball stars. I was literally frightened out of my sense when I went through Goose Hollow. Once a Goose Hollowite made me promise to give him a nickel if he didn't hit me, and walked up to my house with me while I got it for him. . . . The strange thing was that when I was cornered, and fought, even a licking wasn't a hundredth as bad as I thought it would be; but I never learned anything from that—the next time I ran away just the same, and suffered the most ghastly pangs of fear.

I wasn't much good at the things other boys were, and their codes of honor and conduct didn't hold me. They felt it, too, and had a sort of good-natured contempt for me. I was neither one thing nor the other, neither altogether coward nor brave, neither manly nor sissified, neither ashamed nor unashamed. I think that is why my impression of my boyhood is an unhappy one, and why I have so few close friends in Portland, and why I don't want ever again to live there.

It must have disappointed my father that I was like that, though he never said much about it. He was a great fighter, one of the first of the little bank of political insurgents who were afterwards, as the Progressive Party, to give expression to the new social conscience of the American middle class. His terrible slashing wit, his fine scorn of stupidity and cowardice and littleness, made him many enemies, who never dared attack him to his face, but fought him secretly, and were glad when he died. As United States Marshal under Roosevelt, it was he who, with Francis J. Heney and Lincoln Steffens, smashed the Oregon Land Fraud Ring; which was a brave thing to do in Oregon then. I remember him and Heney in the Marshal's office guying William J. Burns, the detective on the case, for his Hawkshaw make-up and his ridiculous melodramatics. In 1910 a man came around to browbeat my father into contributing to the Republican campaign fund, and he kicked the collector down the courthouse stairs—and was removed from the marshalship by President Taft. Afterward he ran for Congress, but lost out by a slim margin, mainly because he came East to see me graduate from college instead of stumping the state.

When I was 16, I went East to a New Jersey boarding school, and then to Harvard College, and afterward to Europe for a year's travel; and my brother followed me through college. We never knew until later how much our mother and father denied themselves that we might go, and how he poured out his life that we might live like rich men's sons. He and mother always gave us more than we asked, in freedom and understanding as well as material things. And on the day my brother graduated from college, he broke under the terrible effort, and died a few weeks later. It has always seemed to me bitter irony that he couldn't have lived to see my little success. He was always more like a wise, kind friend than a father.

Boarding school, I think, meant more to me than anything in my boyhood. Among these strange boys I came as a stranger, and I soon found out that they were willing to accept me at my own value. I was in fine health. The ordered life of the community interested me; I was impressed by its traditional customs and dignities, school patriotism, and the sense of a long settled and established civilization, so different from the raw, pretentious West. My stories and verses were published in the school paper; I played football, and ran the quarter-mile, with very good average success; I had a fight or two, and stuck it out. There were perilous adventures, too, when a few of us stole down the fire escapes at night and went to country dances, slipping back to bed in the dormitory at dawn. With the school social butterflies, I "fussed" girls in the town, and was not laughed at. Busy, happy, with lots of friends, I expanded into self-confidence. So without trying I found myself; and since then I have never been very much afraid of men.

In 1906 I went up to Harvard almost alone, knowing hardly a soul in the University. My college class entered more than 700 strong and for the first three months it seemed to me, going around to lectures and meetings, as if every one of the 700 had friends but me. I was thrilled with the immensity of Harvard, its infinite opportunities, its august history and traditions—but desperately lonely. I didn't know which way to turn, how to meet people. Fellows passed me in the Yard, shouting gayly to one another; I saw parties off to Boston Saturday night, whooping and yelling on the back platform of the street-car, and they passed hilariously singing under my window in the early dawn. Athletes and musicians and writers and statesmen were emerging from the ranks of the class. The freshman clubs were forming.

And I was out of it all. I "went out" for the college papers, and tried to make the freshman crew, even staying in Cambridge vacations to go down to the empty boat-house and plug away at the machines—and was the last man picked off the squad before they went to New

133

London. I got to know many fellows to nod to, and a very few intimately; but most of my friends were whirled off and up into prominence, and came to see me no more. One of them said he'd room with me sophomore year—but he was tipped off that I wasn't "the right sort" and openly drew away from me. And I, too, hurt a boy who was my friend. He was a Jew, a shy, rather melancholy person. We were always together, we two outsiders. I became irritated and morbid about it—it seemed I would never be part of the rich splendor of college life with him around—so I drew away from him. . . . It hurt him very much, and it taught me better. Since then he has forgiven it, and done wonderful things for me, and we are friends.

My second year was better. I was elected an editor of two of the papers, and knew more fellows. The fortunate and splendid youths, the aristocrats who filled the clubs and dominated college society, didn't seem so attractive. In two open contests, the trial for editor of the college daily paper and that for assistant manager of the varsity crew, I qualified easily for election; but the aristocrats blackballed me. However, that mattered less. During my freshman year I used to *pray* to be liked, to have friends, to be popular with the crowd. Now I had friends, plenty of them; and I have found that when I am working hard at something I love, friends come without my trying, and stay; and fear goes, and that sense of being lost which is so horrible.

From that time on I never felt out of it; I was never popular with the aristocrats; I was never elected to any clubs but one, and that one largely because of a dearth of members who could write lyrics for the annual show. But I was on the papers, was elected president of the Cosmopolitan Club, where 43 nationalities met, became manager of the Musical Clubs, captain of the water-polo team, and an officer in many undergraduate activities. As song leader of the cheering section, I had the supreme blissful sensation of swaying two thousand voices in great clashing choruses during the big football games. The more I met the college aristocrats, the more their cold, cruel stupidity repelled me. I began to pity them for their lack of imagination, and the narrowness of their glittering lives—clubs, athletics, society. College is like the world; outside there is the same class of people, dull and sated and blind.

Harvard University under President Eliot was unique. Individualism was carried to the point where a man who came for a good time could get through and graduate without having learned anything; but on the other hand, anyone could find there anything he wanted from all the world's store of learning. The undergraduates were practically free from control; they could live pretty much where they pleased, and do as they pleased—so long as they attended lectures. There was no attempt made by the authorities to weld the student body together, or to enforce any kind of uniformity. Some men came with allowances of $15,000 a year pocket money, with automobiles and servants, living in gorgeous suites in palatial apartment houses; others in the same class starved in attic bedrooms.

All sorts of strange characters, of every race and mind, poets, philosophers, cranks of every twist, were in our class. The very hugeness of it prevented any one man from knowing more than a few of his classmates, though I managed to make the acquaintance of about 500 of them. The aristocrats controlled the places of pride and power, except when a democratic revolution, such as occurred in my senior year, swept them off their feet; but they were so exclusive that most of the real life went on outside their ranks—and all the intellectual life of the student body. So many fine men were outside the charmed circle that, unlike most colleges, there was no disgrace in not being a "club man." What is known as "college spirit" was not very powerful; no odium attached to those who didn't go to football games and cheer. There was talk of the world, and daring thought, and intellectual insurgency; heresy has always been a Harvard and a New England tradition. Students themselves criticized the faculty for not educating them, attacked the sacred institution of intercollegiate athletics, sneered at undergraduate clubs so holy that no one dared mention their names. No matter what you were or what you did—at Harvard you could find your kind. It wasn't a breeder for masses of mediocrely educated young men equipped with "business" psychology; out of each class came a few creative minds, a few scholars, a few "gentlemen" with insolent manners, and a ruck of nobodies. . . . Things have changed now. I liked Harvard better then.

Toward the end of my college course two influences came into my life, which had a good deal to do with shaping me. One was contact with Professor Copeland, who, under the pretense of teaching English composition, has stimulated generations of men to find color and strength and beauty in books and in the world, and to express it again. The other was what I call, for lack of a better name, the manifestation of the modern spirit. Some men, notably Walter Lippmann, had been reading and thinking and talking about politics and economics, not as dry theoretical studies, but as live forces acting on the world, on the University even. They formed the Socialist Club, to study and discuss all modern social and economic theories, and began to experiment with the community in which they lived.

Under their stimulus the college political clubs, which had formerly been quadrennial mushroom growths for the purpose of drinking beer, parading and burning red fire, took on a new significance. The Club drew up a platform for the Socialist Party in the city elections. It had social legislation introduced into the Massachusetts Legislature. Its members wrote articles in the college papers challenging undergraduate ideals, and muck-raked the University for not paying its servants living wages, and so forth. Out of the agitation sprang the Harvard Men's League for Women's Suffrage, the Single Tax Club, an Anarchist group. The faculty was petitioned for a course in socialism. Prominent radicals were invited to Cambridge to lecture. An open forum was started to debate college matters and the issues of the day. The result of this movement upon the undergraduate world was potent. All over the place radicals sprang up, in music, painting, poetry, the theatre. The more serious college papers took a socialistic, or at least progressive tinge. Of course all this made no ostensible difference in the look of Harvard society, and probably the clubmen and the athletes, who represented us to the world, never even heard of it. But it made me, and many others, realize that there was something going on in the dull outside world more thrilling than college activities, and turned our attention to the writings of men like H. G. Wells and Graham Wallas, wrenching us away from the Oscar Wildean dilettantism that had possessed undergraduate litterateurs for generations.

After college Waldo Peirce and I went abroad as "bull-pushers" on a cattle-boat, for a year's happy-go-lucky wandering. Waldo rebelled at the smells and the ship's company, and jumped overboard off Boston Light, swimming back to shore and later taking the *Lusitania* to Liverpool; meanwhile, I was arrested for his murder, clapped in irons and brought before an Admiralty court at Manchester, where Waldo turned up in the nick of time. I tramped down across England alone, working on farms and sleeping in haymows, meeting Peirce in London again. Then we hoofed it to Dover and tried to stow away on a Channel steamer for France—and got arrested in Calais, of course. Separating, we went through northern France on foot, to Rouen and Paris, and started on a wild automobile trip through Touraine to the Spanish border, and across; and I proceeded into Spain alone, having adventures. I spent the winter in Paris, with excursions around the country, letting it soak in. Then I came home to America to settle down and make my living.

Lincoln Steffens recommended me for a job on *The American Magazine*, where I stayed three years, reading manuscripts and writing stories and verses. More than any other man Lincoln Steffens has influenced my mind. I met him first while I was at Harvard, where he came loving youth, full of understanding, with the breadth of the world clinging to him. I was afraid of him then—afraid of his wisdom, his seriousness, and we didn't talk. But when I came back from France I told him what I had seen and done, and he asked me what I wanted to do. I said I didn't know, except that I wanted to write. Steffens looked at me with that lovely smile: "You can do anything you want to," he said; and I believed him. Since then I have gone to him with my difficulties and troubles, and he has always listened while I solved them myself in the warmth of his understanding. Being with Steffens is to me like flashes of clear light; it is as if I see him, and myself, and the world, with new eyes. I tell him what I see and think, and it comes back to me beautiful, full of meaning. He does not judge or advise—he simply makes everything clear. There are two men who give me confidence in myself, who make me want to work, and to do nothing unworthy—Copeland and Steffens.

New York was an enchanted city to me. It was on an infinitely grander scale than Harvard. Everything was to be found there—it satisfied me utterly. I wandered about the streets, from the soaring imperial towers of downtown, along the East River docks, smelling spices and the clipper ships of the past, through the swarming East Side—alien towns within towns—where the smoky flare of miles of clamorous pushcarts made a splendor of shabby streets; coming upon sudden shrill markets, dripping blood and fishscales in the light of torches, the big Jewish women bawling their wares under the roaring great bridges; thrilling to the ebb and flow of human tides sweeping to work and back, west and east, south and north. I knew Chinatown, and Little Italy, and the quarter of the Syrians; the marionette theatre, Sharkey's and McSorley's saloons, the Bowery lodging houses and the places where the tramps gathered in winter; the Haymarket, the German Village, and all the dives of the Tenderloin. I spent all one summer night on top of a pier of the Williamsburg Bridge; I slept another night in a basket of squid in the Fulton Market, where the red and green and gold sea things glisten in the blue light of the sputtering arcs. The girls that walk the streets were friends of mine, and the drunken sailors off ships newcome from the world's end, and the Spanish longshoremen down on West Street.

I found wonderful obscure restaurants, where the foods of the whole world could be found. I knew how to get dope; where to go to hire a man to kill an enemy; what to do to get into gambling rooms, and secret dance halls. I knew well the parks, and the streets of palaces, the theatres and hotels; the ugly growth of the city spreading like a disease, the decrepit places whence life was ebbing, and the squares and streets where an old, beautiful leisurely existence was drowned in the mounting roar of the slums. I knew Washington Square, and the artists and writers, the near-Bohemians, the radicals. I went to gangsters' balls at Tammany Hall, on excursions of the Tim Sullivan Association, to Coney Island on hot summer nights. . . . Within a block of my house was all the adventure of the world; within a mile was every foreign country.

In New York I first loved, and I first wrote of the things I saw, with a fierce joy of creation—and knew at last that I could write. There I got my first perceptions of the life of my time. The city and its people were an open book to me; everything had its story, dramatic, full of ironic tragedy and terrible humor. There I first saw that reality transcended all the fine poetic inventions of fastidiousness and medievalism. I was not happy or well long away from New York. . . . I am not now, for that matter; but I cannot live continually in its heart any more. In the city I have no time for much but sensation and experience; but now I want some time of quiet, and leisure for thought, so I can extract from the richness of my life something beautiful and strong. I am living now in the country, within an hour of town, so I can go down occasionally and plunge into the sea of people, the roaring and the lights—and then come back here to write of it, in the quiet hills, in sunshine and clean wind.

During this time I read a good deal of radical literature, attended meetings of all sorts, met socialists, anarchists, single-taxers, labor-leaders, and besides, all the hair-splitting Utopians and petty doctrine-mongers who cling to skirts of Change. They interested me, so many different human types; and the livingness of theories which could dominate men and women captivated my imagination. On the whole, ideas alone didn't mean much to me. I had to see. In my rambles about the city I couldn't help but observe the ugliness of poverty and all its train of evil, the cruel inequality between rich people who had too many motor cars and poor people who didn't have enough to eat. It didn't come to me from books that the workers produced all the wealth of the world, which went to those who did not earn it.

The Lawrence strike of the textile workers had just ended, and the I.W.W. dominated the social and industrial horizon like a portent of the rising of the oppressed. That strike brought home to me hard the knowledge that the manufacturers get all they can out of labor, pay as little as they must, and permit the existence of great masses of the miserably unemployed in order to keep wages down; that the forces of the State are on the side of property against the propertyless. Our Socialist Party seemed to me duller than religion, and almost as little in touch with labor. The Paterson strike broke out. I met Bill Haywood, Gurley Flynn, Tresca and the other leaders; they attracted me. I liked their understanding of the workers, their revolutionary thought, the boldness of their dream, the way immense crowds of people took fire and came alive under their leadership. Here was drama, change, democracy on the march made visible—a war of the people. I went to Paterson to watch it, was mistaken for a striker while walking the public street, beaten by the police and jailed without any charge. In the jail I talked with exultant men who had blithely defied the lawless brutality of the city government and gone to prison laughing and singing. There were horrors in that jail too; men and boys shut up for months without trial, men going mad and dying, bestial cruelty and disease and filth—and all for the poor. When I came out I helped to organize the Pageant of the Paterson Strike, in Madison Square Garden, New York, drilling a thousand men and women in Paterson and bringing them across New Jersey to act out, before an immensely moved audience of 20,000 people, the wretchedness of their lives and the glory of their revolt.

Since then I have seen and reported many strikes, most of them desperate struggles for the bare necessities of life; and all I have witnessed only confirms my first idea of the class struggle and its inevitability. I wish with all my heart that the proletariat would rise and take their rights—I don't see how else they will get them. Political relief is so slow to come, and year by year the opportunities of peaceful protest and lawful action are curtailed. But I am not sure any more that the working class is capable of revolution, peaceful or otherwise; the workers are so divided and bitterly hostile to each other, so badly led, so blind to their class interest. The War has been a terrible shatterer of faith in economic and political idealism. And yet I cannot give up the idea that out of democracy will be born the new world—richer, braver, freer, more beautiful. As for me, I don't know what I can do to help—I don't know yet. All I know is that my happiness is built on the misery of other people, so that I eat because others go hungry, that I am clothed when other people go almost naked through the frozen cities in winter; and that fact poisons me, disturbs my serenity, makes me write propaganda when I would rather play—though not so much as it once did.

I quit my job to work on the Pageant, and when it was all over I went to pieces nervously, and friends took me abroad for the summer. The strike was starved and lost, the men went back to work dispirited and disillusioned, and the leaders, too, broke down under the long strain of the fight. The I.W.W. itself seemed smashed—indeed it has never recovered its old prestige. I got diphtheria in Italy, and came back to New York weak and despondent. For six months I did almost nothing. And then, through the interest of Lincoln Steffens, *The Metropolitan Magazine* asked me to go to Mexico as war correspondent, and I knew that I must do it.

Villa had just captured Chihuahua when I got to the border, and was getting ready to move on Torreon. I made straight for Chihuahua, and there got a chance to accompany an American mining man down into the mountains of Durango. Hearing that an old half-bandit, half-general was moving to the front, I cut loose and joined him, riding with a wild troop of Mexican cavalry two weeks across the desert, seeing battle at close range, in which my companions were defeated and killed, and fleeing for my life across the desert. I joined Villa then in his march on Torreon, and was in at the fall of that stronghold.

Altogether I was four months with the Constitution-alist armies in Mexico. When I first crossed the border deadliest fear gripped me. I was afraid of death, of mutila-tion, of a strange land and strange people whose speech and thought I did not know. But a terrible curiosity urged me on; I felt *I had to know* how I would act under fire, how I would get along with these primitive folks at war. And I discovered that bullets are not very terrifying, that the fear of death is not such a great thing, and that the Mexicans are wonderfully congenial. That four months of riding hundreds of miles across the blazing plains, sleeping on the ground with the *hombres*, dancing and carousing in looted haciendas all night after an all-day ride, being with them intimately in play, in battle, was perhaps the most satisfactory period of my life. I made good with these wild fighting men, and with myself. I love them and I loved the life. I found myself again. I wrote better than I have ever written.

Then came the European war, to which I went as correspondent, spending a year and a half traveling in all the belligerent countries and on the front of five nations in battle. In Europe I found none of the spontaneity, none of the idealism of the Mexican revolution. It was a war of the workshops, and the trenches were factories turning out ruin—ruin of the spirit as well as of the body, the real and only death. Everything had halted but the engines of hate and destruction. European life, that flashed so many vital facets, ran in one channel, and runs in it now. There seems to me little to choose between the sides; both are horrible to me. The whole Great War is to me just a stoppage of the life and ferment of human evolution. I am waiting, waiting for it all to end, for life to resume so I can find my work.

In thinking it over, I find little in my 30 years that I can hold to. I haven't any God and don't want one; faith is only another word for finding oneself. In my life as in most lives, I guess, love plays a tremendous part. I've had love affairs, passionate happiness, wretched maladjustments; hurt deeply and been deeply hurt. But at last I have found my friend and lover, thrilling and satisfying, closer to me than anyone has ever been. And now I don't care what comes.

1917

3732